DAVID MENON

CHILLING, DARK, AND GRIPPING

"A DSI JEFF BARTON INVESTIGATION"

STORMS

CAN MURDER EVER BE JUSTIFIED?

STORMS

A NOVEL

BY DAVID MENON

Second Edition April 2015

This is for Maddie who is the constant in my life … and it's for all the red shirted men and women I've been working with this summer and our extended Squires Gate family. It's been a blast and I wouldn't have missed it for the world.

This is also for anyone who's never been a blue, calm sea but who's always been a storm.

I'm grateful once again to Paul Barker and his skill that helped me put this revised edition together.

David was born in Derby, England in 1961 and has lived all over the UK but now he divides his time between Paris, where his partner lives, and the northwest of England. In 2009 he gave up a long career in the airline industry to concentrate on his writing ambitions. He's now published several books including the series of crime novels featuring Detective Superintendent Jeff Barton that are set in Manchester and the series of Stephanie Marshall mysteries set in Sydney. He's also created the DCI Sara Hoyland series beginning with *'Fall from Grace'*. When he gets any spare time he teaches English to foreign students, mainly Russians, and works part-time for a friendly low fares airline. His other interests include travelling, politics, international current affairs, all the arts of literature, film, TV, theatre and music and he's a devoted fan of American singer/songwriter Stevie Nicks who he calls the voice of his interior world. He loves Indian food, he likes a gin and tonic that's heavy on the g and light on the t, plus a glass or three of red wine. Well,, it doesn't make him a bad person.

www.davidmenon.com

www.facebook.com/davidmenoncrimefictionauthor

www.amazon.co.uk

STORMS ONE

Leroy tried to struggle against the restraints. He was sitting at one end of what felt like some kind of bench with his legs straddled either side. There was an ice-cold metal pole against his back and a thick metal collar round his neck that prevented him from lowering his head. Something was touching the back of his neck. He couldn't figure out what it was but it also felt like metal of some kind. His arms had been pulled back and his wrists cuffed tightly to the metal pole although his hands had been forced too far apart to be able to touch and that was causing excruciating pain in his shoulders. His knees were bent and his ankles chained to something behind him. He'd been stripped naked and he was cold. He was really cold. Tape had been placed over his mouth and eyes. He could almost smell his own fear.

Then the man's voice filled him once more with horror.

It was a voice he didn't recognise but somehow he knew it was the voice of a white man.

"You may as well save your strength," said the man. "You're really going to need it."

Leroy heard the man step closer and then he lit a cigarette. "Face up to it, Leroy. You won't be getting out of here alive. You've come here to die, my friend. Or rather you've come here for me to execute you. That's when the fun will start. Well, it will for me anyway but for you it might not be so much fun. More like the unbearable torments of Hell. You think you control the streets. You think you can take whatever you want and give absolutely nothing back. Well, let me tell you, Leroy, it isn't going to happen anymore because I'm going to pick you all off, one by one, and teach the Gorton Boys a valuable lesson in 'an eye for an eye'."

The man paused whilst he took a drag on his cigarette. Leroy was breathing rapidly and was totally consumed with terror.

"Do you know what, Leroy? I was so keen to get down here and fill you in on what's going to be happening during your last hours on earth that I forgot to bring an ashtray. Still, there are always other places to stub your fag out."

The man grabbed Leroy's penis, pulled back the foreskin and stubbed his cigarette out on the end. He kept it there, grinding the hot tobacco into the sensitive flesh. Leroy struggled once more in his restrained position. He was desperate to get away from the onslaught of sudden pain and couldn't help crying even though he knew it was useless. He tried to scream but the tape across his mouth muffled the sound.

"Try and get some sleep now, there's a good boy," said the man. "You'll need some rest whilst you contemplate your last night here on this earth."

Leroy was hungry but the need for food and especially water was being savagely repressed by the pain that felt like it was tearing his muscles apart. He'd barely been able to sleep but when his body had given in to the need for some kind of close down he'd immediately woken up again with a start and started crying when he remembered the situation he was in.

It was true that he'd been a pretty bad boy in his time. But the Gorton Boys had been his crew. More than that, they'd been his family and they'd been his future. He'd beaten people up. He'd beaten up young children who'd disrespected the laws of the Gorton Boys. He'd answered them all back and struck fear into their hearts. He'd give anything to be back on those streets now.

Every time he tried to move, even a slight movement of his arms or legs, his body almost seized up with pain. He'd pissed himself. He'd had to. He'd had no choice. He could smell the pool of urine on the floor below him. It was stone cold, wherever he was, and yet he'd been sweating. It felt as if his legs would snap away from the rest of his body at any moment. The ligaments in his shoulders felt like they were on fire as they struggled to keep his arms fixed in their sockets.

He heard the door open and his body almost went into spasm with fear.

"So how was your night?" asked the man. It was the same voice as before. "Sorry. That really was a silly question. I'll shut up and get on with preparing your painful means of death."

Leroy heard the man walk behind him. Oh Christ, what was he going to do to him? He couldn't help pissing himself again.

"Oh, the waterworks," said the man. "Still, I can't say I blame you. You must be terrified. Well, you should be because this is really going to hurt."

Leroy started crying. He could feel the tears roll down from underneath the thick tape across his eyes and across his cheeks.

"I suppose you want your Mum now, don't you? Well, don't worry. You see, I'm filming this whole thing and I'll be sending a copy of the DVD to your dear, sweet mummy. The DVD won't show me of course. I pause the camera when I come into the room. Now, in the best traditions of all executioners, I'm going to let you have your final words."

The man ripped the tape from Leroy's mouth. Leroy let out a groan and was finding it difficult to breathe.

"It's a good job nobody can hear you," said the man. "Now, what do you want to say?"

"Please, man … please don't do this. I'll do anything …."

"Did you give any of your victims the right to a final few words? I don't suppose you did."

"I'm … I'm sorry,"

"Oh, sorry is a bit late, my friend."

"Why are you doing this to me?"

"Because you and the rest of the Gorton Boys have got away with too much for too long."

"I'm begging you, man," Leroy pleaded.

"Oh, this is getting boring!" said the man who then taped Leroy's mouth up again. He watched Leroy try to struggle and got great satisfaction from seeing him twist and contort with frustration and terror.

Leroy heard some kind of mechanism twisting behind him and then the cold metal he'd been feeling against the back of his neck began to move forward and force his neck up against the metal collar. He flinched. He was finding it difficult to breathe.

"Do you know what a garotte is, Leroy? Well, you're strapped to one right now. I turn the wheel at the back here, which forces your neck against the metal collar, and after about four or five twists it'll break your neck and you'll be dead. Each twist will increase the pain you feel and you'll struggle more and more to breathe. Goodbye Leroy. You could've had a truly meaningful life but, as it turns out, your life was pretty pointless really. Better luck next time. Now here's the second twist and, with it, you're just that little bit closer to death."

STORMS TWO

Detective Superintendent Jeff Barton was addressing a meeting of the 'Mothers of the Gorton Boys,' in the Gorton area of east Manchester. The group had been formed after a member of the

Gorton Boys gang, Leroy Patterson, who was only seventeen, had been abducted, murdered, and his body then dumped on the street where he'd lived. The residents wanted to know what the police were doing to catch the killer and were accusing them of neglecting to place all their resources behind the investigation because it was Leroy Patterson, a young black man, who nevertheless had an already-established record of intimidation and violence.

"I can assure everyone here that Greater Manchester Police are conducting their enquiries professionally and without any degree of negativity towards the identity of the victim," said Jeff, emphatically over the loud whispers of discontent. "But, as I said earlier, one of the reasons why we're not getting very far with the investigation is the resistance of this community to talk to us."

An elderly woman stood up and didn't let her years dampen or moderate her obvious anger. "We're talking to you now! But we don't get the meaning of talking when it's not backed up by action."

"But that's precisely why we're not getting anywhere," Jeff countered, although in a calmer, more measured, voice than before. He'd dressed himself up in a suit with a shirt and tie instead of his usual preferred attire of leather jacket, chinos and some variety of check-pattered shirt. He'd thought it essential to look the part with a community where all the ladies in particular took such care of their appearance. "We hit up against a brick wall of antagonism to the police every single time and it makes it very difficult for us to even try and do our job. Leroy Patterson didn't just disappear off the streets. He left the house of his friend Tyrone Peters at 11.30 on the night of the 17th to walk the quarter of a mile to his own house on Millgate Drive. We know he never made it. But someone must've seen something. Someone must've heard something that made them go to their window and sneak a look through the curtains. This is a built-up area with very little open space and I'm just not prepared to accept that nobody saw or heard anything, either then or when his body was left at the end of Millgate Drive two nights later. You notice strangers in this area. Somebody will have noticed someone that night."

Jeff was on a panel with the local Labour councillor for the ward, a man called Royston Albright who lived just a stone's throw behind the community centre where they were meeting. Sitting right in the middle of the 'audience' was the silent brooding figure of Melanie Patterson, Leroy's mother. Jeff had met her when he'd gone to inform her of her son's fate and he couldn't help but find her an attractive woman. Her shiny black hair had been straightened and was at shoulder length. She certainly looked after her figure, which had been accentuated by a tight-fitting black dress, and her make-up was subtle.

On the face of it there was no shortage of suspects when it came to who might be responsible for the abduction of Leroy Patterson. The number of fellow professional criminals with a grudge against the Gorton Boys was as long as your arm, not to mention the ordinary members of the community whose lives had been shattered by the actions of the gang in some way or other. But the use of violence by the Gorton Boys, and those associated with them, was crude and banal. It was entirely physical and locked around fists and crowbars. Whoever had killed Leroy Patterson was in an altogether different league of savagery. According to the pathologist, June Hawkins, Leroy had been killed by suffocation but not with someone's hands. The marks on the back of his broken neck suggested to June that it had been crushed by some sort of a device. And the only thing she could think of was the ancient execution device known as a garrotte.

The estate was sprawled out across a couple of miles to the east of Manchester city centre with the main Sheffield road as its artery and the Etihad Stadium dominating the immediate skyline. The Gorton Boys had taken over the entire area and the local housing association had been inundated with requests, mainly from elderly people who were too scared to go out, especially after dark, to be moved to somewhere else. But spare housing stock was low in most areas and the opportunity to grant the wishes of everyone who wanted to move out was just not possible. So people lived in fear. Local tradesmen making deliveries and workmen putting in telephone lines or fixing boilers always came in two's. None of them would risk going onto the estate alone. Ambulances and fire engines had been regularly attacked whilst they'd been going about their duties and an elderly woman had recently died in the back of the ambulance that was trying to get her to hospital but which had been held up by a mob wielding large planks of wood and iron bars. They'd struck the engine bonnet, the sides and back of the ambulance, terrifying the woman inside in her final moments of life. They gave her no thought or decency but, when they got fed up, they finally just let the ambulance pass. It was all a game of power to them. They didn't care who got hurt as long as it wasn't them. The woman died before she reached the hospital.

"When have you ever helped us?" somebody cried out.

"And when have you ever accepted our help in good faith?" Jeff retorted. The room suddenly went quiet. He could see the ladies and gentlemen of the press who were in attendance suddenly sit up and take notice. They're not interested in justice for anyone. They just want the angle of a white police officer losing his rag with local residents in a predominantly West Indian community. That's what they'd be looking for. And now he was about to hand it to them on a plate. "Look, it's time for a dialogue between us based on truth and honesty. I'll grant you that the police have sometimes been at fault in the past but I don't accept that it's all the fault of the police. It goes both ways and I will hunt down the killer or killers of Leroy Patterson and I will lead a team to the best of our collective responsibility. But I need something from you. I need to know the names of everyone who was part of the mob that surrounded the ambulance that prevented Evelyn Squires from getting to the hospital promptly after her heart attack. Evelyn Squires died. But you know that. You also know that the mob that surrounded the ambulance she was in was responsible for her death. It wasn't the police and it certainly wasn't those brave paramedics. But you won't give us any names, will you? You expect us to do our job, and rightly so, but if it's one of yours, you let them get away with murder. And then you wonder why relations between us are so bad? Do you not see what I'm getting at here? Justice is not a one-way street. It means we have to talk to each other if we're going to solve the murder of Leroy Patterson and find out who the cowards were who prevented Evelyn Squires from getting to the hospital. But, as you accuse me and my colleagues of dragging our feet in relation to the death of Leroy Patterson, you should remember that this community has got the highest rate of gang-related crime in this city but, if you allow yourselves to get to know me, you'll realise that the very last thing anybody could accuse me of is racism. The law is the law whether you're a black teenager in a gang or an elderly white woman on her way to hospital. Think about it and work with me."

Jeff sat down and breathed out slowly. There was silence in the room. He hadn't expected to make that kind of speech but he thought it was necessary and perhaps overdue. He was sick and tired of the police taking all the knocks when half the time they'd be able to solve many more crimes if the public were open and frank with them. He was also sick and tired of people expecting him to be a racist just because he was a police officer. If that was the game they wanted to play then they most certainly had picked on the wrong one. It would no doubt get him into trouble with the powers that be on the force but so be it. Chief Superintendent Chambers would no doubt be calling him in to explain the press headlines that would undoubtedly follow but he was prepared for that. He looked at his watch. It was just before nine o'clock. He wanted to get home to see his son, Toby, who'd been off school with measles. Jeff had taken some time off earlier in the week to be with him but their live-in housekeeper and child minder Brendan had been doing a wonderful job and Toby was over the worst now. He'd probably be back at school in a day or two. In the meantime, he had his iPad to keep him occupied and a multitude of films that Brendan had downloaded for him to watch whilst his temperature came down and the spots on his skin began to disappear.

It was clear from the way people were turning their backs on the panel that they considered the meeting to be over. Royston Albright began gathering his things together.

"That was a good speech, Jeff," said Royston. "But if I'd have made it, I'd lose my seat at the next election. I'm a member of this community so I speak as one who knows that they don't like having it given back to them."

"I was quite tempered compared to what I really wanted to say, Royston," said Jeff. "Maybe I'll save the rest for next time but I've got to convince them to trust me. Surely it can't be that impossible?"

"Well, you never know," said Royston. "They did put a man on the moon after all."

Jeff smiled. "You'll keep me posted if you hear anything?"

"Of course. I've got your number. We'll keep in touch. I'm not your enemy, Jeff. I support you in what you're trying to do."

"Thanks Royston," said Jeff, who was then collared by members of the press. He told them he had nothing to add to what he'd said in his speech and to what he'd said earlier that day in the press conference. As for whether his strident tone would win him more enemies than friends, he said that was too early to tell but that he had an investigation to conduct and he and his team would be getting on with that. Once they realised they weren't going to get any more gold out of him they lost interest and transferred their efforts to what remained of the audience. Jeff noticed that most people were standing round Melanie Patterson, who gave him the odd backward glance that didn't look friendly. She was probably in her early forties and Jeff admired the way her chocolate-coloured skin contrasted with the deep red of her nail polish and lipstick. He watched her put on a thick overcoat. He thought that maybe it was time to start looking towards the future where relationships were concerned. Up until recently he hadn't been able to even entertain the idea of being with another woman. He certainly found this woman attractive but he could never entertain the idea of getting involved with the mother of a murder victim. It just wouldn't be right on so many levels. But to establish some kind of positive rapport with her might be useful in unlocking the community resistance to police enquiries.

"She's the one woman in this community who you really do need to have on your side," said Royston, who'd been kept back by the journalists and then seen where Jeff's eyes were focusing. "She's like an unofficial leader. The rest of them listen to what she says. Of course, there is talk about what kind of role she really plays in this community."

"How do you mean?" Jeff asked.

"There are stories, rumours," said Royston. "They say that she's always been the real power behind the Gorton Boys."

"Really?"

"Oh, yeah," said Royston. "They've made her out to be a proper Winnie Mandela at times. Now, I don't know for sure and I wouldn't like to speculate beyond what I've already said but it might be worth your while persisting with her."

"I think I'll try and talk to her again," said Jeff. He jumped off the makeshift stage and stepped briskly over. The rest of the people dispersed as he approached.

"Excuse me?" said Jeff. "Mrs Patterson? Could we have a word?"

Melanie Patterson didn't look at him as she replied. "I suppose you think that was a fine speech you made?"

"Well, it wasn't scripted."

"And it sounded to me like it was driven by your ignorant prejudice about this community. Talk to you? Listen to you? I'd rather die."

"No, I'm sorry, I'm not going to let you get away with that one."

"I beg your pardon?"

"What you just said to me was not only wrong but it was unpleasant and deeply offensive. Now, I know you're grieving but if I didn't care about what I was doing and if I wasn't being genuine then I wouldn't have come down here tonight and I wouldn't have said any of those things."

"So what are you saying?"

"That we've got more in common than you think."

"So you say."

"Why can't you work with me? Don't you want us to find the killer of your son?"

Melanie gave out a short laugh. "You think I'm going to agree to collusion with the enemy?"

"For the sake of finding your son's killer then, yes, I do."

"Do you have children?"

"What?"

"It's a simple enough question."

"Yes I do. I have a son. His name is Toby."

"And I suppose Toby is being taken care of tonight in your nice big house in your nice white suburb by your nice pretty wife who doesn't have a care in the world?"

"Actually my nice pretty wife died almost two years ago of an aneurism that exploded in her brain. She was only thirty years old. I'm a single dad and both father and mother to my son. It's not always easy. So, do you want to make any more judgements about me and my family when you know nothing about my life?"

Melanie was embarrassed "I'm sorry to hear all that. A young man like you shouldn't be left with a child to bring up on his own."

"It's no more or less difficult than it is for a woman left in the same circumstances," said Jeff. "It's called 'life' and you have to get on with it. And I'm trying to reconcile here the fact that you love to judge others but won't be judged yourself. How do you work that one out? And why is it that you think the only prejudice is against black people?"

"Because it is,"

"Well, let me tell you something. My wife was of Chinese heritage and do you know where the racism in our life came from? It came from my own parents, who never accepted Lillie Mae because she was Chinese and who never come anywhere near their grandson because he's mixed race, even though he's lost his mum at such an early age and could do with knowing that they love him. So don't lecture me about racism, Mrs Patterson, because I know all about it at first hand."

"I'm sorry again."

"You don't have to be. I know that you know about it too. But black people don't have the monopoly."

"You do speak frankly for a police officer. I'll give you that."

"I really think it might help if we talked sometime, MrsPatterson," said Jeff.

"But I blame the police for my son's murder and that includes you."

"That's not fair, Mrs Patterson. Your son was part of a gang that terrorised people in this community and you have the nerve to stand there and blame the police for his murder?"

"Well, if you really want me to think differently then find my son's killer," Melanie struck back. "Then I might be prepared to believe that you're genuine and we might be able to talk."

"We'll need to talk way before then if we're going to really help things around here," said Jeff. "You already have my card from when I came to see you before. Call me."

Melanie picked up her handbag and threw it over her shoulder. "I'll think about it."

"That's all I can ask."

"You'll keep me informed about the investigation into my son's murder?"

"You do believe there is one going on then?"

Melanie smiled. "Alright, I'll give you that one. Well,, I'd better be going."

"How are you coping?"

"I lost Leroy's father to cancer five years ago. I don't cope, Mr Barton. I get through each day as best I can but I don't need to explain that to you because you know what it feels like to lose someone close."

"Good days and bad days."

"Exactly. And I was just getting over the loss of my husband when life dealt me this new blow."

"I think you should call me Jeff."

"And I suppose you can call me Melanie."

"So, will you call me so we can talk?"

Melanie smiled. "I said I'd think about it and I will think about it."

STORMS THREE

"So now, with regard to the Leroy Patterson case," said Jeff, who was sitting in his office with DI Rebecca Stockton. "I wanted to sound you out, Becky, about the initial statement by Melanie Patterson, mother of Leroy?"

"Well, to be honest, sir," said Rebecca. "I've never heard such sanctimonious twaddle in all my life."

Jeff gave a half smile. "Don't sit on the fence now, Rebecca."

"Well, sir, her son had been a thug and yet she was talking about him as if he'd found the secret to achieving world peace. She claims to have been devoted to him as his mother and yet all that devotion led to him becoming a member of a gang that terrorised people. Leroy left school a year early without any qualifications to do anything with his life other than engage in criminality. I've read his school reports. They all say he was lazy and had too much attitude to focus on his education but, of course, according to his oh-so-devoted mother, it was none of her or his fault. It was all the fault of the rest of us."

"I take it you're not too keen on her then?"

"Her hypocrisy hit me like the smell of someone wearing dirty underwear."

"Right, well, I think I'll go and see her on my own in that case," said Jeff.

"Are you saying I can't be professional and keep my private opinions to myself, sir?"

"No, I'm not saying that, Becky," said Jeff who was slightly taken aback by the sudden aggression in Rebecca's tone.

"Well, with all due respect, it sounds like it to me," said Rebecca who was seriously annoyed at Jeff's attitude.

"Look, the important thing here is to build trust in the community to help solve the case," said Jeff. "And you'll need to put your feelings to one side in order for us to do that."

"I'm well aware of that, sir," said Rebecca, testily. "I'm hardly a rookie recruit."

"Right," said Jeff, who wondered what the hell had got into Rebecca. "I'm glad that's settled. Look Becky, I don't know what gets into you sometimes but you've got to stop this moodiness of yours. Sometimes I don't know who the hell you're going to be from one day to the next, whether you're going to be the excellent police officer and someone I regard as a close friend, or whether you're going to be this stroppy teenager who keeps throwing her toys out."

"Is this an official bollocking, sir?"

"You see, there you go again. Becky, we've got two new officers joining the team today. I don't want them walking into an atmosphere of tension between the two senior officers so buck your ideas up. And that's an order."

Rebecca looked at Jeff and wondered if he was genuinely in denial or just plain stupid. "I'll see the Leroy Patterson case through to its conclusion, sir. And then I'll apply for a transfer to another team."

"Rebecca, I ... "

"You just don't see it, do you sir?" she blurted out, more emotionally than she'd wanted to. "You just don't see it."

"What don't I see?"

"That it's ... that it's better for the integrity of the squad if we don't work together."

"You've got to say more than that after dropping that bombshell."

"No sir, actually I don't have to say anything else."

"I may not accept your transfer request."

"Then I'll go to the Police Federation."

"Oh, Becky for God's sake ...."

"And sir, if you don't mind, it's DI Stockton from now on."

Jeff drove onto the Gorton estate and pulled up outside Melanie Patterson's house. Earlier, he'd had another exchange of words with Rebecca about whether or not she should accompany him on the visit. He didn't like falling out with any of his officers and he had thought that Rebecca was more of a friend than a colleague and could therefore get past any short circuits in their working relationship. Perhaps he was wrong. So much tension had crept into their relationship over recent weeks and he'd clearly got under her skin about something, which was why she was intending to transfer from his team. But he also had to remember that he was her boss and, if she continued to speak to him the way she had been doing, then another, and far more ugly, issue might have to be addressed. Jeff had never thrown his rank around. He'd never needed to. His management style had always led to his team co-operating with him and not challenging him for the sake of their egos. This may be one of those times when he needed to be a lot firmer about just who was in charge. They say that familiarity breeds contempt. He didn't really hold with that but he wouldn't have the piss taken out of him just because people think they can on account of his less-than-fervent style of authority. But something was driving Rebecca's oscillating moods and he would never accept any transfer request until he knew what that was. His brother Lewis had often said that it was as clear as day that Rebecca was in love with Jeff. But Jeff didn't see that. He and Rebecca were too close as friends for there to be anything else involved and, besides, he just didn't feel that way about her. At least, he didn't think he did.

After he'd got out of his car, he didn't have to look in order to know that suspicious eyes were falling on him from everywhere. Curtains were parting, doors were being opened and people were appearing to see who the stranger in their midst was. Some of them would remember him from the Town Hall meeting but some of those would've been determined to forget. But that didn't matter to Jeff. He wanted to know how a killer had come onto this estate, snatched a member of the controlling gang and then dumped his dead body back here a couple of days later. Did Leroy Patterson know who his abductor was and go with them willingly, not knowing the trap he was being led into? Was somebody here helping whoever it was? Was it someone from inside who had their own reasons for turning on the Gorton Boys? There were plenty of questions Jeff needed answers to and he had to get people round here to talk if he was going to find the killer of Leroy Patterson.

The inside of Melanie Patterson's modest former council house was absolutely immaculate. It was one of those houses where you are a little bit afraid to sit down in case you disturb the perfect arrangement of cushions. It didn't look like there was a thing out of place and everything had been cleaned to within an inch of its natural life. The front window didn't have any of the marks of residual cleaning liquid that some people's windows have and, as she talked, Melanie was constantly fiddling with something. Either she was straightening the already perfectly-hung curtains or running her hands over the cushions, even though they didn't need it. Then, between all that, she picked up bits of fluff that Jeff couldn't actually see from the carpet. She was wearing a soft grey blouse and a pair of black trousers that had both been perfectly pressed. She was a lady who liked to keep up appearances and that can't be easy when you live on benefits. None of the things Jeff saw around him looked like they'd come from the cheaper end of the market.

"Remind me, Leroy did live here with you, Melanie?" asked Jeff.

"Indeed he did," said Melanie with a slight smile in Jeff's direction.

"He hadn't moved out then?"

"No, he was born in this house and I took him to the cemetery from this house."

"But I understand you don't live here alone?"

"No, I still have my miracle child."

"Your miracle child?"

"About fifteen years ago, there was a massive hurricane back home in St. Kitts," she explained. "The death toll ran into three figures. My brother and sister-in-law perished and the authorities had initially assumed that their son had perished too, poor child. He'd only have been five years old then. But just two months ago, my nephew Jackson Williams turned up on my doorstep, as large as life. He'd been rescued during the hurricane and put into an orphanage and, last year, he decided to track down his family. He found out about his old Aunt Melanie in Manchester, England. So he came over here and I welcomed him into my home. It was as if the good Lord knew that I was going to be lonely."

"Where is Jackson now?"

"He's out and that's all you need to know," said Melanie, a little sharply. "Sorry. It's just hard for me to separate the man from the police officer when I talk to you. Jackson has been a great comfort to me these past few days since I lost my son to a murderer. Have you got anywhere with your … investigation?"

"I'm afraid not, Melanie," Jeff admitted. It was true enough. They'd drawn a complete blank in their enquiries. "Look Melanie, I really need your help here. I've listened to talk, here and there, and I know that people in this community look to you for leadership."

Melanie put on a half-smile. "Not always in a good way, as far as the police are concerned. I've been harassed by your fellow officers on more occasions than I care to remember."

"Well, let's park that for the moment," said Jeff. "Melanie, there's so much we need to know if we're going to make any headway with this investigation but all we've had so far from conducting door-to-door enquiries down this street and those around it are the doors slammed in our faces. You can see how that makes our job difficult."

"I suppose you've got a point," said Melanie, who, despite herself, couldn't help but like this tall white man with the dark blond hair and the sparkle mixed with sadness in his eyes that were a reflection of her own. "Don't you think it hurts me if my friends and neighbours know something that they're not passing on to you?"

"Then help me, Melanie. You won't be betraying anybody but it might start something that will lead to us getting justice for Leroy."

"I'll talk to people round and about," said Melanie. "I'll do my best."

"And what about Evelyn Squires?"

"What about her?"

"I need the names of those who stopped her ambulance getting through, Melanie," said Jeff. "And I'm equally as determined on that as I am about getting justice for your son."

"I can't promise you the Earth, Jeff," said Melanie, who was in a dilemma when it came to the incident with the ambulance. Nobody was going to drop their own kid in it but she needed Jeff on side to get whoever had taken Leroy. "But you'd better come back in a couple of days with the rest of them you need to do your work and I'll try and make sure the doors aren't slammed in your face."

"That's as much as I can ask, Melanie," said Jeff. "Thank you."

"You're welcome."

"Why do so many young men join the Gorton Boys, Melanie?"

"You don't ask easy questions, Jeff," said Melanie. Her heart was heavy with the loss of her son but she had to keep on protecting him. She was his mother. "You see, Jeff, the young people round here feel as far away from the bright lights of the city centre just down the road as they do from somewhere like America. They don't feel part of the great modern success we're all being told that Manchester is. They feel they have no control of anything to do with their destiny except these streets."

"There's no excuse for the kind of violence we've seen from the Gorton Boys, Melanie."

"It's what they feel, Jeff."

"And I hear white youths in other areas articulating the same problems, Melanie."

"Well, maybe they don't have the cards stacked against them like our boys do."

"Melanie, how do you think they get in that state in the first place? They live on estates that are in a far worse condition than I've seen round here."

"Me and the rest of the women take pride in our neighbourhood and like to make it look nice. But when it comes to our boys, the rest of society has rejected them and expects them to fail."

"Yes, and they prove those cynics right," said Jeff. "They play into their hands. Look Melanie, I'm a mere police officer. I can't change the world. All I do is uphold the law with due fairness to everyone. But if this community can start working with us instead of believing we're part of some grand conspiracy against you then we can start to turn things round."

"Will the alleged wrongdoings of the Gorton Boys be placed in the past so that we can move on?"

"You're talking about immunity from prosecution?" Jeff questioned. He was surprised she'd been as blunt as that and, from an intelligent woman such as her, it wasn't what he would have expected. She was chancing it. She knew what the answer would be and yet he was also surprised at how relatively co-operative she was being, considering how belligerent she'd been previously. What was motivating this turn around? Jeff didn't allow himself to think that it was just his charm.

"Yes," said Melanie. "How else could we move on?"

"That's way beyond my remit, Melanie, and something I just couldn't promise you or even comment about."

"Just as I thought," said Melanie. "At least you're honest and I admire that in a man. Now, shall I make us some tea?"

"Only if it's not too much trouble, Melanie."

Melanie stood up. "When you're a mother who's buried her child, nothing seems to be much trouble."

"I can understand how that feels," said Jeff.

"You lost your wife. That's how you can understand. You were a husband and I was a mother who devoted herself to her child instead of going off and chasing a career like so many women do these days. They neglect their children."

This was where Jeff had sympathy with Rebecca Stockton's perspective on Melanie Patterson. If she'd been the mother of all mothers, as she claimed to have been, then how come her son did end up a mindless thug? She was deluded. It was part of being a mother in the middle of gang activity on some of Manchester's toughest streets. Melanie Patterson had to believe that she'd done everything right. It was the only truth she could hold onto. But could it be, like Royston Albright had said, that Melanie did actually play a significant role in the activities of the Gorton Boys?

"You hold some strong views, Melanie."

"I'm a woman of traditional values, Jeff."

Jeff wondered what shape those traditional values took, as he sat waiting for Melanie to return with the tea. When she did come back, everything that was presented was pristine as Jeff had expected. The silver spoons, the bone china cups and saucers, the matching teapot, sugar bowl and milk jug.

"It must be hard for someone with the kind of job you're in to bring up a child on their own," remarked Melanie as she handed Jeff his tea. "But surely there must be someone else in the picture? A good looking man like you wouldn't be short of suitors."

Jeff smiled. "You make me blush, Melanie."

"I speak as I find."

"Well, if there are, then I'm not good at reading the signals."

"You've closed down that side of yourself."

"Probably."

"Then it's about time you turned it back on again."

"Now you really are making me blush, Melanie," said Jeff. "Tell me, did Leroy have a girlfriend?"

"No," said Melanie, firmly. "He did not."

"You seem pretty sure about that."

"You asked me the question and I gave you the answer," said Melanie. "And just when the conversation was starting to get interesting. I'm lonely, just like you, Jeff. And I know what it's like to lose the one you love."

"Look, Melanie, you're a very attractive woman and I'm flattered by the attention but I have to keep things professional between us," said Jeff. There was no way anything could happen between him and Melanie Patterson. She could end up being a suspect. "I should go, Melanie."

"I understand," said Melanie. "With all your talk of professionalism, you know you've got to move on and yet you don't want to let go of the past either."

Jeff breathed in deep. She was right and yet she was also so very wrong. "Thank you for the tea. I'll be in touch."

As soon as Jeff was gone Melanie's back door opened and her nephew Jackson Williams came in. Melanie took the tray of tea things back into the kitchen.

"Well,?" Jackson questioned.

"Well, what, young man?"

"Has the copper gone?"

"Yes, he's gone," said Melanie who placed the tray down on the kitchen table before turning to Jackson.

"So you've finished trying to make out with him?"

Melanie was incensed by the way Jackson sometimes spoke to her. "I will do whatever I can to find my son's killer and don't you forget that if you want to stay under my roof. Now, have you found anything out?"

"No," Jackson replied. "Nothing at all."

"Well, that's just not good enough! Now get back out there and keep on sniffing. Because if the police find Leroy's cheap little white slut of a girlfriend before I do then you'll really see what I'm capable of. She caused my Leroy's death. And one way or another she's going to pay."

Before Jeff left the estate, he decided to have a look at Evelyn Squires' house. It was only a couple of streets away from Melanie Patterson's and he wanted to get his bearings. But when he got there, it looked like it had been hit by a bomb.

The front door was falling off its hinges. He stepped inside and was immediately confronted by a tall dark haired white man in his mid to late forties, dressed in blue jeans, training shoes and a brown casual leather jacket. There was also a woman of about the same age looking anxiously at him from inside the living room.

"So who the fuck are you?" the man demanded. Jeff could see he'd been crying but the tears had clearly turned into a sharp anger. His voice also carried a slight accent that wasn't local.

Jeff held up his warrant card. "I'm Detective Superintendent Jeff Barton and …."

The man threw up his arms in despair, turned and walked back into the living room, stepping over the mess as he went. "The police? What a fucking joke!"

"Sir, would you like to calm down and tell me who you are?"

The man turned but said nothing. Then the woman spoke.

"John, please give him your name," she implored, with the same accent as her husband. "He might be able to help."

The man took a second or two and then spoke in a much softer voice than before. "I'm John Squires. This is my wife Antonia."

"And Evelyn Squires was your mother?"

John nodded.

"Yes, she was," Antonia confirmed. "She was John's mother."

"Mr and Mrs Squires, I really am very sorry for your loss."

"Thank you, Detective," said Antonia. "But if Evelyn's death, in the circumstances it happened, wasn't bad enough, we come here this morning and find that her house has been broken into and looted." She put her hand to her mouth and was clearly holding back the tears. "It's so cruel."

"Have you called 999?"

"What a stupid waste of time that would be," John sneered. "You've no control over these streets. Somebody should come in here and show them just who's the boss but, because of all the politically-correct bullshit, everybody is too scared to confront the truth. It wouldn't have happened back home in the old days before the rest of the world made us go soft."

"John, would you please stop swearing," said Antonia.

"I'm sorry," said John. "But there isn't much left for me to express how I feel."

Jeff used his mobile to call the incident in and then carried on talking to the Squires. "My colleagues will be here as soon as they can to take statements from you." He looked round at all the mess. "Is everywhere in the house like this?"

"Her bedroom is even worse," said Antonia. "Then there are windows broken everywhere. All her possessions ransacked and most of them stolen."

"Including her ring," said John. He wiped his big hand over his mouth. "My father gave her that eternity ring before they got married. She'd only taken it off because of the arthritis in the joints of her fingers. Now it's gone forever."

Antonia crossed the space between her and her husband and rested her head on his shoulder in a gesture of comfort.

"We begged her to come and live with us," John continued, holding his wife's hand. "We live down in Cheadle and there's enough room upstairs for us to have built her a Granny flat. But she was proud. She was so bloody proud and where did it get her?"

"Mr Squires, I can assure you that I, personally, am determined to bring what happened to a just conclusion," He handed them his card. "Please call me anytime and I'll respond to you. I'll also keep you informed of any progress in the investigation."

Antonia smiled. "Thank you, Detective."

"I have no faith in the police, Detective," said John. "I'm sure you mean well and you'll do all you've been trained to do but the fact is, like I said before, you have no control of these streets. The black youths write their own laws and run bloody rings round you."

"John, that's enough, darling," said Antonia.

"But it's true, Toni."

"Mr Squires, you talked before about 'back home'?" said Jeff, who was struggling to keep his patience against such a blatantly racist onslaught. He put it down to the man's grief exploding all the rest of his emotions. "Where were you talking about?"

"My family emigrated to Rhodesia long before the country was handed over to that evil thug Mugabe. He ended up taking our farm off us. We lost everything. Then my father died and my mother got sick so we came back so she could use the NHS. But she didn't recognise her own country anymore. So many different bloody races everywhere. It appalled her. She hated what her country had turned into, with all the traditional values gone and everything ruled by Brussels. If you don't get whoever did this to my mother, Detective, then, believe me, I will."

Jeff began to wonder if all this bluster from Squires was hiding something else. Could he have been involved in the murder of Leroy Patterson? He certainly had the motive and his rage was clear and understandable. But would he be as blatant as to come back onto the estate when somebody could have recognised him?

"I would strongly advise you not to take the law into your own hands, Mr Squires," said Jeff. "You know what the consequences of that would be."

"You do your job, Detective," said Squires. "And I won't have to."

STORMS FOUR

Back in the old days he'd been 'well in' with the council. All the lads who worked for them were. But it was all so different now. It was all so different. Most of them down at the council wouldn't know him beyond a reference number and wouldn't care either.

The two ulcers on the side of his leg were being troublesome little bastards. They weren't big but they knew how to shoot pain through him like an automatic charge of electricity and boy, oh boy, they itched as if they were being used to torture him.

Monica was his Community Nurse. She came round to attend to patients like him who couldn't get down to the clinic. A little on the large side but Monica was a decent English girl. She wasn't some freeloading foreigner. He could understand her and she could understand him. She'd make a good matron when the time came.

"So how are you today, Ralph?" asked Monica as she began to set up her things on the floor beside his feet.

"Well, once you've dressed my blessed ulcers I'll be fine for at least half an hour until they drive me mad again with itching."

"I'm going to apply a different cream today and I'm confident you'll be itch-free for longer than you've been used to," said Monica. "Are you taking care of yourself otherwise?"

"Well, at over eighty years old, I am thinking of giving up the dancing girls of an evening," said Ralph. "I was getting bored with that whole scene anyway."

Monica laughed. "I'll bet you were one for the ladies in your day, Ralph." She took off his shoes and socks and held her breath. There was always a rancid smell from his exposed feet. "You've still got that gleam in your eye."

"You flatter me, Monica. Just like I expect your husband could flatten me if he thought I was flirting with you."

"He's not the jealous type I'm happy to say," said Monica as she wiped her hands. "I couldn't cope with a husband like that."

"Monica, can you do me a favour?"

"Of course, if I can. What is it?"

"I need you to post me a letter."

Monica frowned. "Is it to the police?"

"Yes, and don't look at me like that," said Ralph. "It's my duty as a citizen to report what I see and I know I'm just a stupid old man who they probably won't listen to but I've got to try."

Ralph's flat was on the first floor of a housing association building on the other side of the main road from the entry slip road into the Gorton estate. It gave him a panoramic view of much of the estate and a vantage point that would be the envy of anyone trying to control it. He was surprised that nobody had noticed and come to see him. He would have been prepared to accept any offer for his silence. He wasn't so daft as to not take advantage of the modern way of doing things round here and they say Barbados would be a lovely place for someone who hasn't had a holiday for years. But nobody had noticed and, even if they had, they hadn't been to see him. So that's why he was turning to the police.

"Ralph," Monica began, on her knees beside his chair. "Think about this. You could potentially be bringing a whole load of trouble on yourself."

"I don't care."

"But you should care, Ralph. It could be very dangerous. Who knows what they might do if they found out it was you."

"I'm doing my civic duty, Monica. This letter is important."

"Ralph, I'm scared of the repercussions. Don't you see what I mean?"

"You shouldn't be scared. I'm not. I'd be going out with some sort of a bang to make up for the unremarkable life I've had."

Ralph had been too young to see action during World War 2 but he had done his National Service and that's where he'd met Edith. She'd worked in the dining hall where the soldiers had all their meals on the base where they were stationed. She used to clear the plates and glasses and wash them up in the kitchen. She'd caught Ralph's eye and, one day, he'd plucked up enough courage to ask her out. She'd said 'yes' and within a year they were married. They moved into a council house in Denton when Ralph returned to Civvy Street and they had two daughters. Ralph never got a sense that Edith was desperately unhappy. She never wanted to go anywhere. Ralph got about because of his job driving vans for the council but he went beyond the borough. Edith always said she was happy at home and even when Ralph talked her into a week's family holiday in Rhyl, they had to come back on the Tuesday because Edith was missing her 'little home'. The girls sided with their mother, like they always did, and even when Edith left Ralph for an insurance salesman with a much bigger private, detached 'little home' in Clitheroe, they still took their mother's side. Now he only sees them when they drop in a week before Christmas with a card and a bottle of whisky. They always watch the door and look at the clock every couple of minutes as if they can't wait to leave again and they make all manner of excuses as to why they can't have him for the festive season. He'd never understood what he'd done to make them so distant. He'd been a good father and provided for them as much as he could. He'd taken an interest in their schoolwork and what they were doing. He'd never hit them or treated them badly in any way. But still they'd given all their affection to their stepfather who had money and who ended up seeing far more of Ralph's grandchildren than he ever did.

"At least I'd know something would be happening in my otherwise stale and boring old life," Ralph went on. "What difference would anything else make?"

Monica could feel her heart breaking. She knew what Ralph meant but she really didn't think he'd weighed up the possible consequences of what he wanted to do. She'd seen what they do on the Gorton estate. It was like a war zone in parts of it.

"So will you post my letter, please, Monica?"

Monica put the letter in her pocket and smiled. She had no intention of posting it. If Ralph couldn't see where it could all lead, she could and she had to protect the poor old man. "Okay," she said. "Seeing as it's you."

Annabel Matheson had been through Hell these past few months. Everything that could have gone wrong for her had gone wrong and she wished she could step back in time to when she first discovered boys and life had held such promise. Now she was a failure. Forty-two years old, without a penny in the bank, and not even owning the roof over the head of herself and her son. It had been a sudden plunge into darkness. She'd gone from being the socially upwardly-mobile wife of a very British small businessman to being the very socially downward single Mum with a fourteen-year old son to take care of after her husband cleared off, leaving her with thousands of pounds worth of debt to clear. She should have known it would turn out this way. Her now ex-husband Clive had gone bankrupt once before. She'd stood by him then. Everything to do with his building business and all his bank accounts and credit cards had all gone into Annabel's name and he'd carried on with nothing on the surface to show that he was an undisclosed bankrupt. She'd been happy to show him the faith that no bank would because, despite the doubts that had been slowly growing inside her head, she was still in love with him and was blinded by her affections. It had taken a visit from the bailiffs at six in the morning, when they'd taken everything but the kitchen sink, to finally bring her to her senses. That and the fact that Clive had used the opportunity to tell her he was leaving her for one of the barmaids at the local pub with whom he'd been having an affair for months. At least he'd done all the damage in one go.

Annabel now worked as a receptionist at the Carrington Hotel on Blackpool's North Shore. It was one of the few four star hotels in the resort and, although she found the work easy and sometimes a lot of fun, the office politics that went with it were sometimes so bloody exasperating. The hotel General Manager, Marilyn Kent, who everybody nicknamed 'The Ice Maiden' because of her avoidance of anything remotely human like a feeling, was adored by some and reviled by others because of the way she controlled the staff, especially the front line receptionists, according to how your face fitted with her. It had absolutely nothing to do with someone's ability to do their job. If promotion was on offer then she'd make sure that one of her 'golden boys' got it regardless of whether or not they were competent. She was very Thatcherite and didn't promote women. She only liked to promote and surround herself with men so that she could be the focus of all attention. Annabel had been leapfrogged for promotion twice by men who weren't as good at their job as she was but she'd never been a 'brown nose' in her life and wasn't going to start now. And there was no point in complaining. Marilyn was only interested in the hotel's financial results. She was about as interested in the people management side of the business as she was in drinking her own piss. If a staff member had a grievance, they were made to sweep it all under the carpet and put on the smile of a happy team that gets results. She basically couldn't have cared less about the feelings of her staff. She occasionally wafted down from her office upstairs to dispense the shallow talk she considered to be wisdom and to remind staff of the hotel group's current financial targets. She was in competition with the hotel group's other properties in Leeds, Manchester, Newcastle, and Glasgow - and she liked to win. It's said that she only got the job by providing one of the hotel group directors with oral sex. Annabel could well imagine that, because the job was way beyond Kent's obviously limited abilities.

Annabel drove down from her rented house which was a block back from the promenade in the Anchorsholme district of the nearby seaside town of Cleveleys to start work on the 7 o'clock morning shift. She needed the car. Early starts and late finishes didn't always fit in with public transport, even though the famous Blackpool tramline passed right by the hotel. She was about ten minutes early and so allowed herself a cigarette which she smoked with the car window open. Her son Kyle was always giving out to her about her smoking. He was turning into a proper little old woman. Bless him. At least he cared about his old mum.

What Kyle didn't know about was his mother's torrid affair with Dermot, who was one of the hotel's maintenance men. He was tall, masculine and, when she first saw him, she thought he'd be the kind of lover who'd throw her round a hotel room and leave her breathless. And indeed he was like that, but she'd also discovered a passionate, sensual side to him that left her even more breathless. Annabel wasn't proud of herself for stepping on another woman's patch but she needed to take just a little something back from life after all she'd lost when Clive betrayed her. She told herself it was all just a bit of fun. It didn't matter that he was doing her self-confidence the world of good after it had taken such a battering. It didn't matter that she went weak at the knees whenever he winked and smiled at her. It didn't matter that he texted her a video of him ejaculating, on one of those days when they couldn't get together to fulfil their carnal needs. It didn't matter that she would never admit to him that he could break her heart. She was pretending that none of it mattered and that she could walk away from it, just like that. It didn't matter that she was deceiving herself.

She finished her cigarette and put a mint sweet in her mouth to help clear her breath. She walked into the hotel and immediately saw Tim Robinson, one of the hotel's temporary summer recruits waiting to take over from the reception night shift. She loved Tim. He was about the same age as her and had matured well, with his full head of black hair and lack of a beer belly. But he was also a bit of a mysterious one. He lived in a one-bedroom flat about ten minutes walk from the hotel and nobody really knew why a man of his age was still doing a reception job and wasn't a manager of some kind. He'd been of working age for a good twenty years and yet appeared to have nothing to show for it. He spoke well and seemed intelligent. And he was also very funny. He made her laugh and could do a blisteringly good impression of Marilyn Kent. He'd clearly been around and could talk about all sorts of things and places and people. But, although he was handsome and eloquent, he never talked about men or women and nobody knew which side of the stamp he licked. And nobody felt comfortable enough to ask him. It was one of those things.

"Hello you!" he greeted her and they exchanged a kiss on each cheek.

"Hello yourself," said Annabel, who was so pleased they were going to be working together. "Why didn't you let me pick you up this morning? It looked like it might've rained. You'd have got wet."

Tim stared at her. Annabel had seen that look before. He was like a rabbit caught in headlights and he didn't know which way to jump to avoid being run over. What was that all about?

"Oh, I felt like the walk," said Tim, who then added a smile. "I was almost here by the time you sent me the text."

"Oh, right," said Annabel, nodding but not knowing whether to believe him or not. Well, of course she believed him. Why on earth would he lie to her about something so meaningless? "Well, I'll give you a lift home once we're finished anyway."

"Thanks," said Tim, his smile remaining. "That would be great."

Tim and Annabel then took the briefing from the night receptionist. Annabel knew that Tim would take it all in and end up being *de facto* in charge and she was quite happy about that so she let her eyes wander. No matter how hard they tried, the hotel still attracted a good eighty odd per cent of its clientele from the usual crowd of 'chav' families – although these were the upper end of the 'chav' market who no doubt lived in houses with bay windows – and old people who'd never even contemplate going abroad because nowhere abroad served proper tea. It was depressing to look out at them all sometimes. Annabel rarely saw anyone who was half decent to look at. Thank Christ for Dermot, when he wandered through in his overalls from fixing this or that. She could feel herself getting wet at the thought of him. Then she turned back to who was giving Tim the morning briefing. Jane was a miserable bitch. Mid-forties, not married and didn't everybody know about it! Anything that had ever happened to you, she'd had ten times worse and she often had a set face that could curdle milk at a glance. She was also the staff trainer which she thought gave her some kind of added authority. She'd been promoted by Marilyn Kent because, Annabel considered, she was ugly and therefore no threat to Marilyn getting all the men's attention. Annabel silently scolded herself. Jane wasn't ugly. It was unfair of her to think that but she did have a downtrodden disposition, with a long face to match, that made her ugly. She was also Marilyn's little pet because anything anybody ever told Jane went straight to Marilyn. She couldn't be trusted as far as any of them could spit and, yet, if anyone exposed her for wearing more faces than the town clock she threw such a drama with endless tears that everyone ended up feeling bad and dropped all charges even though they knew they were true. And Marilyn, of course, always believed Jane's lies above anyone else's truth.

"So what have you been up to on your days off?" asked Annabel after Jane had finally gone home. Well,, she'd left the reception desk to call in on Marilyn Kent before going home.

"Oh, this and that," said Tim in that way he had of telling you everything and yet nothing at all. "Relaxing mostly. Watching some TV, catching up on the laundry."

"I thought you were going to call me to meet up?"

"Well, I was," said Tim, feeling himself go red and a little hot. "I was. I seriously was. But I just seemed to run out of time."

"Okay, I'll forgive you," she chided. "But next time we have the same day off, I'm going to insist we do something."

"Yes, boss!"

"Which reminds me," said Annabel. "I don't mean to pry or anything, Tim, but do you have any family anywhere? You never speak of any."

"I have a brother," said Tim. "But we're not close and we don't see each other."

"That's a shame."

"Is it?"

"Well, he is your brother."

"You don't know him like I do."

"Ah, like that is it?"

"We're very different people," Tim revealed. "And I don't know why family members who don't get on are made to feel like they should keep on trying just because they carry the same blood."

"Oh, I wasn't suggesting that, I …"

"I know you weren't, don't worry, I didn't think that. I was just talking generally, you know."

Annabel looked up and saw Marilyn Kent walking down the ground floor corridor towards reception. She was in her usual striped trouser suit with a black low-cut top underneath, radio in her hand in case she's 'needed' urgently in another part of the hotel..

"Oh, here we go," said Annabel. "Guess who's on her way to us?"

"I thought there was a chill in the air on this bright and beautiful August morning."

"Good morning, boss," said Tim.

"Okay," said Marilyn. "Now before anybody starts, I'd just like you to know that I come down here for a chat and a break from all I've got on at the moment, so please bear that in mind before you start firing questions at me."

"I only said good morning," said Tim who couldn't stand the stupid cow. Call herself a manager? That's a bloody joke. "So if we were to ask you how the sale of the hotel to the new owners is going, then you wouldn't be able to answer us?"

Marilyn closed her eyes in apparent frustration. "You all know that the hotel group has been bought out."

"But, Marilyn, what we also need to know is the possible impact that might have on our jobs," said Annabel. "You know how I'm fixed. I've got Kyle to think about."

"Yes, I do know that, Annabel," said Marilyn, firmly.

"So you can't tell us anything about the impact on the business that the new owners will have?" Tim tried. "Or even who those new owners are?"

"The identity of the new owners has not been revealed, even to me, yet," Marilyn replied testily. Then she went in for the kill. "But all I do know, Tim, is that none of you temporaries will be kept on beyond the end of the season."

"And could there be jobs for us elsewhere in the group?"

Tim didn't get an answer to his follow-up question because Marilyn's attention was taken by one of her pets from the accounts office who started talking to her about last night's episode of Big Brother which was clearly more important to Marilyn that answering her staff's legitimate questions about the future of their employment.

"How did she get that job?" Tim ruminated, shaking his head.

"That's what everybody wonders," said Annabel.

"Apparently, sir, they heard Melanie Patterson's screams of horror half a dozen houses away," said DS Ollie Wright.

"I'm not surprised," said DI Rebecca Stockton. "I don't like the woman but this is bloody sick."

Melanie Patterson had received a DVD from the murderer of her son, Leroy. It was a film of Leroy being executed and she'd sent it on to Jeff. He and his team had just finished watching it.

"I've never seen anything like that," said DS Adrian Bradshaw, shaking his head. "The poor bastard. What was that thing he was strapped to?"

"It's called a garotte," said Ollie. "It's a medieval method of execution that was mainly used by the Spanish right up until the time of Franco in the sixties and seventies."

Everybody looked round quizzically at Ollie.

"Look, I took my niece and nephew to Blackpool at the weekend and we went in this dungeon place by the Tower where they have all this stuff to do with ancient torture and execution methods. They have actors scaring the living daylights out of people too and it was quite good fun actually. Our Charlotte and Jason enjoyed it and so did I."

"I'm glad that's the explanation, Ollie," said Jeff, who was thinking how distraught Melanie Patterson would be after watching that. "We've got some really twisted individual to find here, if that's not an understatement after watching that film, and we've got to make significant progress before he gets the chance to do that to someone else."

"We've got as many of the routes in and out of the estate covered with either CCTV or uniform surveillance, sir," said Rebecca. Although she'd hardened her heart towards Jeff in the way of romance, it had only been to protect herself from any further heartache. She still wanted to support him implicitly as her senior officer and regretted the previous spat they'd had. Life was increasingly becoming about the separation between work and personal life. She wished it wasn't that way but neither did she feel she had any choice than to accept that it was and it was why she still intended to go through with her transfer request. "Short of closing off the estate completely, there's not much more we can do on that score and it still means that someone could get in there without us noticing."

"True," said Jeff. He avoided letting his eyes linger on Rebecca anymore. The tension between them had given way to an obvious distance that sometimes pissed him right off. Why couldn't they go back to where they were before? Was he so weak and pathetic that he couldn't bring himself to talk to her about the situation between them? He didn't ask to be widowed at thirty-four years old with a young son to bring up. He was doing the best he could but he hadn't bargained for the loss of his beloved wife to emotionally regress him by about fifteen years. "So where else can we go for answers?"

"Well, at least the community is now talking to us, sir," said Ollie. "Even though they're not telling us much, they're not slamming their doors in our faces anymore."

"Can we go through everything from the house-to-house on the estate, please," said Jeff. "I know there's precious little there but I want you to go back to anyone who told us anything, however small or insignificant it might appear. There's got to be some way of tying something together to make a lot more than it first seems. Now Ollie, what did you find out about Melanie Patterson and her nephew Jackson Williams?"

This wasn't a question that Ollie was comfortable about answering. He needed to speak to the boss about this in private but, in the meantime, he decided to share the official story about Jackson Williams. "A background check on Jackson Williams confirms what Melanie Patterson told you, sir, orphaned in a hurricane, lived in a children's home before coming to stay with his aunt here. And, on the face of it, his aunt must be supporting him because he has no visible signs of any other income."

"Unless he's living off the immoral earnings of the Gorton Boys," said Rebecca. "Like I suspect Melanie Patterson is too, because her only visible means of financial support is the benefits she gets. But from what you said about her house, sir, she must be getting money from somewhere else. It would be my guess that she's more involved with the Gorton Boys and all their rackets than she'd like us to know and I would put money on her knowing something about the looting of Evelyn Squires' house."

"Then bring her in," said Jeff.

Rebecca looked round in silent surprise before turning her eyes back on Jeff. He'd seemed protective of Melanie Patterson up until he'd been to see her. Rebecca wondered what she'd said to make him change back into an investigating police officer and away from the pathetic alpha male he came across as when the name of Melanie Patterson was mentioned. "Do you mean that, sir?"

"Why wouldn't I mean it, DI Stockton? Leroy's funeral was yesterday and. even though we kept a discreet distance. we were never going to pick up anything from it. I know you think, or thought, that I was a little blind where Melanie Patterson is concerned but you were wrong and you've been wrong all along. I'm not blind to what she really might be up to and I'm not soft on her because her son was brutally murdered. I'm still a police officer, DI Stockton. First and foremost I want a result and whatever I think about Melanie Patterson is worth nothing compared to that. Is that understood?"

Rebecca swallowed. She hadn't counted on Jeff being quite so forthright. "Loud and clear, sir."

"Good," said Jeff. "Now let's get on with it."

Ollie waited for the room to clear before approaching Jeff. "Can I have a word, sir? In private."

STORMS FIVE

"What's on your mind, Ollie?" Jeff asked. There was just the two of them and the door was closed. He wasn't necessarily in the mood for emotional complexities. He hoped to God that Ollie had a problem of the operational kind.

"Well, if I'm right, then it could be as wrong as it gets, sir," Ollie answered. "You asked me to look into the background of Jackson Williams…."

"Yes, and you gave the team your answers during the briefing."

"Well, it isn't quite as simple as that, sir, which is why I wanted to talk to you privately about it because you'll know what to do if I'm right and, if I am, then the fewer people who know the truth, the better."

Jeff gestured for Ollie to sit down in front of his desk. "So are you saying that what you said in the briefing isn't true?"

"No," said Ollie. "What I said was the truth as we're meant to believe it."

"You'd better explain,"

"Sir, when the pictures of Jackson Williams came through I was immediately struck by something," Ollie went on. "I recognised him. I was a speaker at an Association of Black Police Officers dinner a few months back. The man we know as Jackson Williams was there and he asked me a lot of questions about advancing in the force as a black officer. I remember he was very ambitious and I got the feeling he'd do anything to get ahead. His name was Tyler Moore, sir. That's Police Constable Tyler Moore and I suspect that he's working undercover with the Gorton Boys."

Jeff knew all about undercover operations and the obvious need to keep information about them to the tightest circle of officers as possible. But if the identity of this undercover officer had been blown then that would have consequences.

"Ollie, I don't doubt anything you say but you'll understand that we could've picked ourselves up a bomb here," said Jeff. "Do you have any other means of proving that the man known as Jackson Williams and living with his aunt Melanie Patterson in Gorton is not who he says he is?"

"Yes, sir," said Ollie, who understood exactly why his boss had asked the question. "I did some further digging on Jackson Williams. It's true that his parents died in the hurricane and Jackson was placed in a local orphanage. But the real Jackson Williams was adopted a couple of years later and he emigrated with his new family to the US soon after. They live in Philadelphia."

"And you can prove this, Ollie?"

"Conclusively, sir."

"Okay," said Jeff. "Then leave it with me and, I know I don't need to ask, don't breathe a word of this to anyone until you and I have spoken again about it."

People who play games instead of being honest with themselves and the world about their true feelings are just weak. That was the conclusion Tim had drawn from years of slaying the demon of his own desires, day after exhausting day. His position was somewhat different from all the others though. Nobody, not even his new best friend Annabel, would be able to guess that ever since the fire that almost killed him, all those years ago, he'd been trapped inside a prison that meant that he didn't have the choice but to be strong. .

"So do you think they'll keep you on at the end of the season?" asked Annabel after she'd sat down in the coffee shop. They'd arranged to meet outside of work because Annabel saw that as a gesture of real, proper friendship that existed beyond the end of each shift. She'd had to really pin Tim down about it. He'd managed to slither his way out of two previous arrangements they'd made and that morning she'd checked her mobile for text messages a dozen times. She'd been sure he would back out again with some lame excuse. But, no, this time he was sitting opposite her with his caramel latte looking spick and span in his short leather jacket, white T-shirt and blue jeans. He looked younger than he did in his uniform at work. But then he looked young anyway. There were few lines on that handsome face. Surely someone must be keeping him warm at night.

"You'd have to ask our glorious leader, Marilyn Kent, that," said Tim.

"Leader? She doesn't lead anything except her own targets, whether it's to do with the job or her own taste for wine."

"Well, I wasn't being desperately serious."

"No, but Suzie was yesterday."

Yesterday Tim and Annabel had attended the celebratory lunch for Suzie, one of the reception staff who was leaving because her husband had got promotion at work and because that meant he'd be doing a lot of travelling they'd decided that Suzie would give up her job. After all, they didn't need the money anymore and someone needed to be at home during regular hours for the kids. A good lunch in one of Lytham's finest restaurants had been enjoyed by all and when even more wine had appeared to cater for those who'd reached the point where enough was not enough, Marilyn Kent, who'd got herself rather more pissed than the rest of them, decided to grant proceedings her pearls of wisdom.

"Now that he's got you as the pretty little stay-at-home wife bringing up the kids for him, it won't be long before he's off shagging," Marilyn had declared, leaning tipsily across the table and trying to get right in Suzie's face.

Suzie, who was known for not taking any nonsense off anyone, but who'd had more than one disagreement with her boss, had been waiting to bat it straight back to Marilyn. So she'd taken a deep breath and whilst everyone looked on in silence she said "No, he won't, Marilyn. And do you know why? Because he's married to me and not to you."

Marilyn's face had been a picture.

"She delivered a classic reposte," Tim recalled, smiling.

"Oh, it was worthy of Krystle and Alexis in Dynasty," said Annabel, remembering every moment. "Did you ever watch Dynasty?"

"Only until someone went up in a space ship," said Tim. "That's when it all got a bit too daft for me."

"She's very good at it."

"Maybe so but she's not an actress," Tim countered. "Not really. She can deliver lines but only as herself."

Well,, thought Annabel. If he is gay, he can't be that gay. All the gays love Joan Collins. Or so she thought. They all love that kind of bad tempered diva. But perhaps there were varying degrees of someone being gay? Perhaps it was more of an *a la carte* menu than an uptake of the full menu option. She'd often thought about this. In the old days, it was all about Larry Grayson and John Inman and the things that were now being found out about the likes of Liberace. With today's openness it wasn't surprising when the most macho of men turned out to be gay. And that was good. But where would Tim place himself along this newly-liberated line of ordinary men who happen to be gay.

"Did you enjoy yourself at the lunch yesterday?"

"That was a change of subject bolt out of the blue!"

"Well, you know me," said Annabel. "What comes into my head tends to exit straight away through my mouth."

"Well, didn't I look like I was enjoying myself?"

"Yes, you did but …. "

"But what?"

"I don't mean to interrogate you, Tim."

"Then don't."

"But it's just that I feel I know you, and yet I think I don't really know you. I don't mean that in any kind of malicious or critical way."

Tim smiled. If only she really did know him. "But you've got your meat and potatoes Irishman. Isn't that enough man for you?"

Tim relished being surrounded by wholesome family men like Annabel's Dermot at work. They were all tall and broad and had wives or girlfriends to go home to. They had houses onto which they built extensions. They went on package holidays to Spain or Greece or Turkey. They had extended families with whom they spent Christmas and birthdays. They'd learnt about sex when they were teenagers and were experienced enough to show their wives or girlfriends a good time. . They expected mortgages, kids, a house in the suburbs. They expected to sit around and moan and whine about inconsequential bullshit without ever doing anything constructive to change the situation . They condemned their women for gossiping and yet the wholesome men themselves were the biggest gossips. Tim would like to join them sometimes. He'd love to know how it really felt to have stepped onto the treadmill of ordinary life with such apparent ease. He'd known so long ago that he'd never be able to achieve something so fulfilling.

"Well, I'm thinking about knocking all that on the head," said Annabel.

"What? Dermot?"

"Yeah."

"Why?"

"Because his wife is a psycho and would probably beat me up if she found out."

"You mean someone as good looking as Dermot would have a wife like that?"

"You do recognise that he's good looking, then?" said Annabel, sensing a way through the armour around Tim's senses.

"Even other men would see that Dermot had a sexiness about him, Annabel."

"Interesting," said Annabel, who still didn't know if she was any the wiser about what made Tim tick in the groin department. "But back to Dermot. I'd be cutting my nose off to spite my face if I did finish with him because he's got such stamina and we have the most fantastic sex."

"He looks like he would be strong in that department."

"There you go again."

"What?"

"Telling me a little and then no more."

"We're all a puzzle though aren't we?"

"Well, I'm not," said Annabel. "Not where my sexuality is concerned."

"And you think I am when it comes to that?"

"I don't know what to think about you, Tim."

Just at that moment when Tim was wondering what he could say next to continue confusing her, she got a text from Dermot saying he was going to be free all day on Saturday and asking if they could they get together. She told Tim about it.

"But I can't," she said with a long face.

"Why not?"

"Because of Kyle."

"Well, I'll take care of Kyle," Tim offered.

"Really?"

"Sure," Tim confirmed. "He has met me before."

"Yes and he liked you."

"Well, he's a nice lad and a credit to you," said Tim. "I could take him to the Pleasure Beach whilst you're creating your own pleasure beach at home."

"Are you sure? Fourteen year old lads can be difficult. I mean, I'm lucky with Kyle because he's basically a good lad but he's shy, Tim. He doesn't open up easily to people which was why I was pleasantly surprised when he opened up so easily to you."

"Perhaps I've just got the touch."

"Perhaps you should've been a dad."

"Oh, I don't know about that," said Tim. "I've got to grow up a lot myself before I could even consider that. But look, Kyle and I will be fine. You can have your good time and I'll make sure Kyle has a day to remember."

"I can't believe you're willing to do this for me," said Annabel, who was close to tears. Not even her own family, such as it was, had offered her any help with Kyle since Clive left them. "You're such a nice man, Tim."

"Hey," said Tim. "It's what friends are for."

Chief Superintendent Geraldine Chambers had a soft spot for Jeff Barton. He was the kind of man she hoped her own son would grow up to be. He was every inch the man but he was modern and full of the values of today. He was sensitive. He gave more than just a passing thought for the welfare of his team and Geraldine liked that. He was the modern kind of police officer. He was himself but with a warrant card. Her son had been on her mind a lot lately. There wasn't much chance of him growing up to be as open-minded as Jeff judging by how much poison his father had poured into his head about Geraldine. She'd never wanted to hurt her ex-husband. That had been the very last thing she would ever have wanted. But he considered the fact that she'd left him for another woman to be a sin that was not worthy of his forgiveness. If he knew the kind of problems she was now having with her partner, Sheila, it might please him in some way that she was suffering. But you can't go crawling back to someone you've hurt and expect them to offer you sympathy and support because the one you left them for gets a bit too handy with her fists.

"Jeff, I think you already know Detective Chief Inspector Mike Phillips who heads up the unit dealing with gang crime in the city," said Geraldine once Jeff had joined her and Mike in Geraldine's office. "Please take a seat, gentlemen."

Jeff and Mike shook hands in that very alpha male way, characteristic of when two officers meet. To reflect Jeff's higher rank Mike addressed him initially as 'sir," but Jeff told him to dispense with formalities.

"I don't need to tell you ,Jeff, that we have a situation to deal with in relation to PC Tyler Moore," Geraldine went on. "And it needs to be dealt with fast."

"Mike, just how did you come to place a rookie PC in the middle of a potentially very dangerous undercover operation?"

Mike noted the slight rebuke in Jeff's voice but he'd been prepared for it. Looking back, it maybe wasn't his best decision to put Tyler Moore in with the Gorton Boys but it was too late to waste time on regretting that now.

"Tyler Moore is an extremely able young police officer," said Mike. "He came to my attention during an operation involving a Salford gang in which he put his life on the line in the arrest of the gang leader who was wielding a sawn-off shotgun and was more than ready to use it on a police officer who he considered as the enemy. If you don't mind me saying, Tyler Moore is far beyond being labelled as a rookie. He's intelligent and very capable."

"I don't doubt any of that, Mike, but surely you must have assessed the risks of putting him in there?"

"I did," said Mike. He shifted in his seat. He was feeling somewhat defensive. "And, whatever happens, it is on my head. I accept that."

"Tyler Moore has been able to provide Mike with a lot of valuable intelligence regarding the activities of Melanie Patterson, Jeff," said Geraldine.

"Go on," said Jeff.

"Well," said Mike. "Melanie Patterson is the undisputed leader of the Gorton Boys. Sure, it was made out that her son, Leroy, held the top spot but he couldn't do anything without consulting his mother first. The Gorton Boys used a mixture of violence and intimidation to control what they considered to be their streets and they made a lot of money from the drugs trade on the estate. They'd also started a new line in pimping. Girls, boys, usually addicts, who'd do anything to get enough cash for a fix."

"Nothing new in that," said Jeff. "It's more or less classic."

"True enough," said Mike. "But make no mistake, Jeff. Melanie Patterson ruled the Gorton Boys with a rod of iron. We knew all about the intimidation and the drugs and the pimping but the reason why I put Tyler Moore in there as her long-lost nephew was so that he could find evidence linking her to two murders eighteen months ago. The bodies of two former members of the Gorton Boys, Alan Chaplin and Reggie Clayton, were found on waste ground to the side of the A580 East Lancashire Road.. The pathologist concluded that they'd been burned, probably whilst still alive, and because of the way their skin had burnt and the residue of rubber around their necks, heads, and shoulders, it looked like they'd been 'necklaced'. Tyler was able to find out that it had been done because the two victims had been suspected by Melanie Patterson of having talked to the police about the Gorton Boys activities."

"And had they?"

"They'd both approached us but we hadn't been able to talk to them before they were murdered. But it was enough to convince me and fellow officers that they'd been got at before they'd had the chance to talk to us."

"It certainly looks that way."

"Now, Melanie Patterson and the rest of the community on the Gorton estate have remained tight-lipped about the murders of Chaplin and Clayton which gave us more reason to believe that our theory was correct."

"With all due respect," said Jeff. "Why am I only hearing about this now?"

"It was vital with regard to protecting the operation and protecting PC Moore, Jeff, that we kept silent," said Geraldine. "Something could've easily leaked out that we had someone in there and he could easily have been fatally compromised once we knew what Melanie Patterson was capable of."

"Okay, point taken, but do we have evidence that Melanie Patterson ordered the deaths?"

"We have her recent admission to Tyler Moore or …to her… her nephew Jackson Williams."

"Then why on earth didn't you pull Tyler out once you'd got what you needed?"

"Because there was still more to find out," Mike responded. "Tyler was gathering evidence on all the names, dates and places that would've made a cast iron case against Melanie Patterson."

"But you are going to pull him in now, surely?"

"I ordered it twenty-four hours ago, as soon as I got word from you that Jackson Williams had been identified as Tyler Moore."

"But I sense there's still a problem?"

"I haven't been able to get hold of Tyler," Mike admitted, a grave look suddenly covering his face. "He's not responding to any of my communications."

STORMS SIX

He'd been careless. He knew that. He should have known better. He'd been a fucking idiot. The man had looked like some kind of delivery driver and called over to him to ask for directions. He was standing at the back of his van, which was parked down a small access street that formed a kind of border between the backs of two rows of houses on the edge of the Gorton estate. Tyler clicked out of being belligerent Jackson Williams and clicked back into being a police officer. He walked over to the man. The back doors of the van were open. The man looked like he was consulting some paperwork that was in his hand and the next thing Tyler knew was a kind of cotton pad was being forced over his mouth and nose. Chloroform. Jesus, how could he have been so stupid? He'd fallen into what was, for a police officer, such an obvious trap. He'd read descriptions of this sort of thing so many times in relation to other abductions. Now he had his own to deal with and the fear was racing through him with an intensity he never thought was possible to feel.

His annoyance at his own failings had stopped him from trying to figure out the reality of his situation. He was naked. There was tape over his eyes and his mouth. He was lying flat on his back and spreadeagled with his wrists and ankles cuffed tightly with no room for him to move his hands or feet by even a small amount. There was some kind of bulky apparatus around his neck that separated his head from the rest of his body and his wrists were attached to what felt like either end of it. What the hell was this sick bastard going to do to him? Leroy Williams had been garotted.

He'd been told about it when he'd reported in to DCI Phillips. He wanted to cry but was determined not to crack for as long as he could hold on. He'd wanted this undercover operation. He'd suggested it and volunteered himself to carry it out. The only way to get the information they needed on the Gorton Boys was to get inside it. He'd discovered a level of criminality that had surpassed his expectations. Melanie Patterson was not someone to be messed with. She was callous and she was cruel. She'd ordered so many beatings of young boys who wouldn't toe the line that she'd lost count. She had no conscience. He'd give anything to be back in her house, arguing with her, right now. He'd give anything to be tucking into his mother's jerk chicken. It was always his favourite. She loved doing it for him. She'd been getting anxious lately because he hadn't been home for a while. God knows what she was going to make of whatever was about to be done to him. How was she going to cope?

He flinched when he heard a door opening behind him and footsteps come close.

"I'm glad you're awake, Jackson," said the man who was standing behind Tyler. "It's so much more fun when the person I'm tormenting is conscious and able to understand the horror of what he's about to go through. I'm enjoying this, you see Jackson. Do you know why I'm doing it? Have you worked out just who I am yet? Or is it beyond your tiny little excuse for a brain?" He took out his packet of cigarettes and got one out. As he was lighting it, he went on. "I started a little ritual with Leroy. I light a cigarette and I stub it out on a part of your body where the pain will be unbearable and then I let you suffer it all night before I come back in the morning to complete your execution." He dragged on his cigarette and then he stubbed it out right on Tyler's neck. He watched as Tyler shifted as best he could to try and quell the pain but it was no good. The man then knelt down so he was close to Tyler's face. "I'm going to get every single one of you until I feel you've paid for what you did. And, even then, I might just carry on. You must be wondering how you're going to be passing from this world and into the next? Well, I'll keep you guessing for now. See you in the morning, Jackson. Hope you have a … restless night."

Tyler hadn't slept at all when the man returned hours later. He had no conception of it being night or day. His neck was so bloody stiff and it ached like hell. The cuffs around his wrists and ankles were cutting into his skin like sharp knives. This must have been what it was like for Leroy. But why was this sick fucker doing this? What did he have against the Gorton Boys? He had to try and keep his mind on rational thoughts for as long as he could or else he could quite literally go mad with terror.

"Good morning, Jackson," said the man as he came into the room. "It's a beautiful day out there. Shame I can't let you see any of it. Shame this is your last day on the old mortal coil. Shame you've been such a bloody useless bastard whilst you've been on this earth. But look, I digress. I've got a lot to do today. You know the usual stuff like shopping, going to the dry cleaners, watching some TV. But first I have to deal with you. Holding your neck in place is a kind of circular cut in a set of stocks which are part of a guillotine. You heard of one of those, Jackson? It's the traditional way the French used to execute people, going all the way back to the Revolution. I can't stand the French personally. All that garlic and snails and frogs' legs. And throughout history, they've never been there when we needed them. But they did devise a quite magnificent way of killing people. And I've added my own little twist especially for you, Jackson. You see, the usual way to place the prisoner for execution was to get them face down with their hands cuffed behind their back. But, as you can tell, I've restrained you on your back with your head facing upwards. That's so, when the time comes, you'll be able to watch the blade come down at rapid speed and chop your head off." He watched as Tyler tried to struggle. "It's no use

Jackson. You won't be able to break free. But I will let you have one final word or two before dying."

The man ripped the tape from across Tyler's mouth and he immediately spoke. "I'm not Jackson Williams. My real name is Tyler Moore and I'm an undercover police officer. I've been undercover gathering information on Melanie Patterson who is the real power in the Gorton Boys gang and who controls everything and everyone. I don't know what it is you've got against them but I'm not part of them, I never have been. I just pretended because of being undercover. Please mate, please let me go. I've done nothing to you. Please! Please!"

The man was incensed. "You mean to tell me that the police had someone on the inside who could've protected ... you rotten little bastard!"

Before Tyler could plead for his life any further, the man angrily ripped the tape from his eyes and Tyler immediately recognised him. Then he looked up and screamed as the man cut the taut rope and the blade was released.

Tyler was dead in seconds. There was blood everywhere.

STORMS SEVEN

Annabel Matheson was sitting on the top of the cliffs opposite the hotel where she worked having a crafty cigarette before starting her shift. It was a beautiful day and, as she smoked, she gazed out over the Irish Sea and wondered where it had all gone wrong because, here she was, at thirty-two with a broken marriage behind her and a lover who was married to another woman. She had her lovely son Kyle and she wouldn't change that for the world but she could do without all the letters that kept arriving on the doorstep demanding money that she hadn't got. She wished she could sleep without having to down a bottle, and sometimes more, of wine a night. She wished those moments with her lover Dermot could last way beyond the time they spent in bed, outstanding as that was. They'd just spent the most wonderful Saturday together when they'd only gone downstairs to get some food and wine out of the fridge which they then consumed back in bed. She'd been depressed after he'd gone home. Her spirits had plummeted through the floor and even her son Kyle had noticed. He had spent what he described as a "fantastic" day with her friend Tim who'd taken him to the Pleasure Beach and then spent a fortune on him with a new pair of jeans and a couple of shirts. It made her feel bad. She knew that Tim didn't earn much. None of them at the hotel did. The place had supposedly been bought out by some other concern but it was still all being kept a secret from the staff. Annabel wished the new owners would declare themselves and start addressing some long-held staff grievances like the peanuts they were paid. Her stepfather had told her to find another job if she couldn't manage. As if it was that bloody easy...... but that was typical of the pig-ignorant bastard. He'd never wasted any sympathy on her, no matter what predicament she found herself in.

It could all have been so different if she'd been allowed to do what she wanted, which was to be an actress. She'd always got her highest marks at school in her drama classes and took the leading role in the annual school play for the last two years she was there. Her performances received glowing praise from teachers, governors and fellow students. But her mother and stepfather never went to see her in her hour of glory and that had really hurt. And they then proved to be an immovable obstacle in the way of her acting ambitions

Her own father had been a married man who her mother had an affair with. He had ditched her as soon as she told him she was pregnant. Then, when Annabel was five, her mother married her stepfather. Right from the start, he made it clear to her that he was never going to replace her father and was only tolerating her because she had to come with her mother. He'd provide for her. He'd make sure there was food on the table and a roof over her head but any love would be reserved for the children he might have with her mother and they subsequently had two. She got on well with her half-siblings, her brother and sister, but her stepfather made it obvious that they had all his love and care and not her. Her mother never seemed to bother that Annabel was always left out of everything as far as her stepfather was concerned. She didn't seem to care that her eldest daughter felt like a stranger in what should have been her family home.

Her drama classes were where Annabel found respite from all the pain and hurt at home. They were her salvation. It was a bit of an old cliché but she could escape from herself by being someone else, even if it was only for a couple of hours a night. It got her through. But her mother and stepfather were adamant. She was to get a job and join all the other followers of 'school, work, marriage, kids, grandkids, death'. They weren't the sort of family who had dreams. They just knuckled down and got on with finding a 'proper' job so that they'd never be a burden on anyone. It had been the first time they'd used the word 'family' when talking about her and that had made her blood boil because it was so bloody unfair. But it was no good. She earned herself a slap across the face for arguing, although not from her stepfather. It came from her mother who told her she should respect her stepfather, the man who'd never even tried to love her. Sometimes she hated her stepfather. But, at other times, she hated her mother even more because she never acknowledged her daughter's pain. It's true what some say about your parents screwing you up. She just prayed to God that she didn't end up doing that to her own son, Kyle.

It wasn't long after she left school that she did the classic thing of many unhappy teenage girls and fell for the first man who showed her any real interest. Clive became her husband and then she was pregnant with Kyle. It was after Kyle had been born that she decided to try and trace her real father. It wasn't terribly difficult. She had his name and where he lived at the time which was in

Oldham. She made contact but it wasn't easy. Her stepmother didn't want to have anything to do with her and she didn't really like her father. She met his other children, his daughter and his two sons and she got on particularly well with the sons, her half-brothers. She's still, sort of, in touch with them. They exchange Christmas and birthday cards but not much else. She doesn't have any contact with her father.

She stubbed out her cigarette and stood up. She straightened down her jacket with the palms of her hands and then turned to walk across the tram tracks and then the road into work. As she was waiting for the 'Fleetwood Ferry' northbound tram to pass, she looked up and saw her friend, Tim, being dropped off outside the hotel. There was nobody else in the car except for the driver who was a man although she couldn't really make out what he looked like. But the car was something else. It was a very flash-looking sports car, a beautiful dark burgundy colour, with a long bonnet and short boot.

"So who was that who dropped you off?" she asked Tim as she walked up to the reception desk where Tim was already making himself at home for the afternoon and evening shift they were about to share.

"What?"

There he goes again, thought Annabel. For a brief moment he looked like some little boy who'd been found out doing something naughty. So she decided to play with it a little.

"Have you been up to no good?" she asked coyly.

"What? Me? No. I most definitely have not."

"So who was the guy in the very nice car?"

"Oh, he's … he's a friend of mine. Just a friend, nothing else. Don't go putting two and two together and making a hundred."

That was it. He closed down. No more discussion of the mystery man in the flash car.

At the end of the shift, Annabel decided to do a little detective work. She was intrigued. She just wanted to know. She called Kyle and told him she'd be a little late back. He was old enough now to be left until she finished the late shift at ten o'clock, just like he could get himself up and ready for school in the morning after she'd left to start the early shift. She sometimes felt guilty about it and worried that she was forcing him to grow up too quickly but what could she do? She didn't actually have any choice since Kyle's father had washed his hands of them both.

At the end of their shift she dropped Tim off at his flat just a few minutes from the hotel. Then, instead of carrying on down to the bottom of the road where she usually turned left towards her place in Cleveleys, she took the next right, turned the car around and parked where she could get a clear view of the door that led up to Tim's flat. It was one of four contained within a large converted Victorian terraced villa on the other side of the road. She knew that this was beyond insane but it wasn't that she didn't trust him as such, it was just that curiosity about this mysterious guy was getting the better of her. Was it a diversion away from her real troubles? Yes, it probably was but she was going to give in to it anyway. Whenever she asked Tim anything about his life it was as if he hadn't got his story prepared. It may be nothing and, if he wanted to keep her at arm's length from his personal life, then that was his business. Nothing wrong with that. But there was something niggling away at the back of her mind that she just couldn't shift. Kyle wanted to spend more time with his new 'Uncle'so she needed some answers and, if Tim wasn't going to give them to her, then she was going to find them out for herself.

She only had to wait a few minutes before the flash burgundy sports car drove up. Tim came out of the flat and got in. Then it drove off and turned round almost in front of where Annabel was parked and headed back towards the promenade. Annabel could see that it was being driven by the same guy who dropped Tim off at the hotel and she followed. Was he his boyfriend? Did Tim think he had to hide his sexuality from her because of Kyle? Well, he'd got to know her well enough now to know that she didn't have a homophobic bone in her body. She would never in a million years stop Kyle from seeing Tim because he was gay.

The sports car turned left at the end and he headed south along the promenade. He carried on all the way through the centre of town, past the Tower and down to where the trams have their southern terminus at Starr Gate. He turned left there, went over the railway bridge, past the airport and, after a couple of miles, he took another left and was going down what was signposted as a 'Private' road. Annabel had never been to this part of town before. She didn't even know it existed. Sure enough it was right on the outskirts of Blackpool but, from the look of all the big detached houses with all their acres of ground, it may as well have been at the other end of the universe from the tackiness of the resort only a few miles away. It was like stepping into another world. There were no street lights and Annabel slowed down before bursting out laughing. This was crazy! What the hell did she think she was doing? It was dark. It was late. Kyle was waiting at home. She suddenly felt vulnerable and conspicuous. Then she saw that the sports car with Tim inside had come to a stop outside the gates of what looked like the largest house along the road, large enough to be called a mansion. Seconds later, the electronic gates opened and the car drove inside before the gates closed behind it.

Annabel reversed her way round a corner and headed back to the main road. She hoped that neither Tim nor his companion had seen her.

DI Rebecca Stockton and DS Ollie Wright were sitting across the interview table from Melanie Patterson.

"You're not helping yourself, Mrs Patterson," said Rebecca.

"I want to speak with Detective Superintendent Jeff Barton," Melanie repeated.

"Mrs Patterson, for the umpteenth time, I've told you that Detective Superintendent Barton is not available, now can we get on with this interview, please?"

"I do not answer the bidding of a stupid white bitch like you!"

"Oh, be my guest and carry on, Mrs Patterson," said Rebecca as calmly as she could, given the provocation this woman was meting out to her. "Your attitude is only making your guilt all the more believable."

"I am guilty of nothing."

"That's not what it looks like to us, Mrs Patterson."

"Well, wherever you got your information from it's wrong."

"Mrs Patterson, did you order the murders of Alan Chaplin and Reggie Clayton?"

"Those names mean nothing to me."

"Oh, come on, Mrs Patterson. They were the sons of neighbours of yours and used to hang out with your own son, Leroy."

"Do not mention my son's name."

"Why don't you want me to mention Leroy's name, Mrs Patterson?"

"Because I buried him only two days ago and you're not worthy to speak his name," said Melanie. She was devastated by having been pulled in for questioning. She'd thought that if she made a connection with Jeff Barton she could avoid ever being under suspicion. Now it just looked like she had been naive. And she hated herself for it. She was also nervous. Somebody must have been talking. Leroy had gone and her nephew Jackson had gone walkabout. Now she was in here, being picked apart by this stupid bitch and the token black police officer whom she considered to be a traitor to his race and history. How any self-respecting black so-called person could join the ranks of the oppressors of their own community was beyond her. "You'll never be worthy to speak my son's name. Do you hear me? Never."

"Well, let's move on," said Rebecca. "Alan Chaplin and Reggie Clayton. Do you still insist you didn't know them?"

"How long are you going to keep me here?"

"As long as is necessary for us to complete our enquiries and I ask again, Mrs Patterson, did you know Alan Chaplin and Reggie Clayton?"

"And I'll tell you again that their names mean nothing to me."

Rebecca took photographs of Chaplin and Clayton that had been taken soon after their bodies had been found and placed them on the table in front of Melanie Patterson. She could see that Melanie tried not to look at them at first but then couldn't help herself and her eyes flickered when she saw the extent of the horror.

"Doesn't make for a very pretty picture, does it?"

"What doesn't?" said Melanie, defiantly.

Rebecca sighed with irritation. "These young men had rubber tyres placed round their necks which were doused in petrol and then set alight. But then you'd know that, wouldn't you Melanie? Because you were there."

"What kind of nonsense are you talking now?" Melanie demanded. If she'd been nervous before she was especially so now. She'd spent so long establishing her position as head of the Gorton Boys and maintaining it by fear. That's why Chaplin and Clayton had been dealt with. They had attempted to betray her and their punishment needed to be shown as a lesson to others who might be tempted to do the same. But what was happening now? It felt like everything was falling apart. And where had her nephew Jackson gone?

"You ordered the murders of Chaplin and Clayton because they threatened your position of power."

"Rubbish!"

"Where does all the money come from, Melanie?"

"What money?"

"The money you use to furnish your house and pay for your twice yearly trips back to the Caribbean? You've never done a day's work in your life. Everything you've done has been by illegal means."

"You don't know what you're talking about," Melanie scoffed. "You're flying on half-baked theories that don't add up to anything significant."

"You ordered their murder."

"I ordered nothing."

"You were afraid they were going to pull the rug from under you and you had them murdered."

"I want to go home."

"That won't be until we've decided we're done with you."

"I'm a citizen and I have rights!"

"So do the residents of the Gorton estate but you didn't seem to respect them."

"I don't know what you mean!"

"I mean the death of Evelyn Squires that could've been prevented."

"And how on God's earth are you trying to connect me with that?"

"Oh, we don't have to try, Mrs Patterson," said Rebecca. "You see, we have names, addresses, times, dates, places. We have all the information we need to make a solid case against you. A case that we can successfully prosecute."

"I need to speak to my lawyer."

"I'm glad you've finally decided to take these matters seriously, Mrs Patterson," said Rebecca. "It can only help you in the long run."

Rebecca brought the interview to a close and then she and Ollie joined Jeff Barton outside in the corridor. Jeff had been watching the interview through the two-way mirror.

"She's on the brink in my opinion, sir," said Ollie. "She's looking decidedly uncomfortable. I don't think it would take much to push her over the edge."

"DI Stockton?" said Jeff. "Is that your assessment too?"

"Yes, sir," Rebecca agreed. "I think Ollie is absolutely right."

They were about to discuss further what approach Rebecca and Ollie would take when they went back in to continue the interview when Chief Superintendent Geraldine Chambers walked up and said she needed a word with Jeff.

"What is it, ma'am?" asked Jeff after he'd gone with Chambers back to her office. DCI Mike Phillips was there too. "Mike?"

"Jeff, we've received a DVD. It's rather disturbing, I'm afraid."

"Disturbing? Is this to do with PC Tyler Moore, ma'am?"

"I think you'd better watch the DVD, Jeff," said Chambers.

Chambers played the video on her desktop computer. It was of PC Tyler Moore being executed by guillotine. It caught all the terror and fear and blood and savagery. There was so much blood that some of it splattered against the camera lens, adding to the extreme horror of the scene.

"It's gut-wrenching," said Geraldine.

"You're not kidding, ma'am," said Jeff who'd had to put his hand across his mouth at one stage of watching the video. It truly was horrific.

"Thank God that because he was undercover his parents have been spared being sent a copy because the killer wouldn't have been aware of who they were," said Chambers. "I have sent a team out to talk to them and give them our support."

DCI Mike Phillips had remained silent so far. Being the officer who sent Tyler Moore into that situation was proving to be a hard cross to bear this particular morning.

"I imagine the press will be on to it, ma'am?" said Jeff.

"Yes, we'll need to hold a press conference, Jeff. I've scheduled it for eleven this morning."

"We're in the middle of questioning Melanie Patterson who thought she was giving a home to her nephew Jackson Williams," said Jeff. "I say we tell her the truth. We expose the whole situation. It isn't going to threaten Tyler Moore, poor sod. But it could push her into an admission of guilt over the matters that Tyler was in there finding out about and smoke out some other members of the Gorton Boys. Mike, is there anything in the intelligence that Tyler Moore gathered that could point to one individual or a group of individuals that could have carried out and had the motive to carry out this horrifying act?"

"The short answer to that is 'no'," said Mike. "We've gone through everything a hundred times. Every encounter Tyler Moore had that he reported back to us. What he did tell us, however, is that Leroy Patterson had a girlfriend. She was a white girl and Melanie Patterson didn't approve. In fact, after Leroy was found dead, she seemed to blame this girlfriend in some twisted way but she'd gone to ground. Nobody knew where she was."

"And do we have an identity for this girlfriend?" Jeff asked.

"I'm afraid not," Mike admitted. "There'd been some problem between them and they weren't speaking at the time of his abduction and subsequent death. Tyler hadn't been in there long enough to find out any more."

Jeff could understand Mike's feelings over the horrendous fate of Tyler Moore but he was becoming more than a little exasperated by his drip feed of potentially useful information. Departmental competition? Christ, when are the police in this country going to get past that load of bloody bollocks?

"Then we'll bring them all in," said Jeff. "Every member of the Gorton Boys will be brought in and I'm keeping Melanie Patterson for as long as I can."

"There is still a risk there though, Jeff," said Chambers.

"There's a risk in everything to do with this, ma'am," Jeff countered. "Tyler Moore paid the ultimate price of that risk."

"And finding Tyler's killer?" asked Mike.

"That's ongoing," said Jeff.

"And we have a potentially very useful piece of information that may carry that part of the investigation forward," said Chambers. "A note came with the DVD." She handed the piece of A4 paper to Jeff and he read it.

ONE BY ONE UNTIL I DECIDE JUSTICE HAS FINALLY BEEN DONE. NICE TRY WITH THE POLICE OFFICER. HE LOST HIS HEAD IN THE LINE OF DUTY AND WAS SO VERY YOUNG. SUCH A SHAME.

"So he's rubbing our nose in it," said Mike. "He's laughing at us."

"Well, maybe not for much longer," said Jeff. "My instincts tell me that the answer to all of this will be found somewhere amongst the rest of the Gorton Boys. And we're going to find it."

STORMS EIGHT

A sombre mood had descended on the police station as might be expected after one of their own had been brutally murdered and his decapitated body dumped on a street on the Gorton estate. Police officers weren't necessarily known for wearing their hearts on their sleeves. They'd seen so much that the rest of society were spared from that it made them immune to public showings of disgust and revulsion. But the killer of PC Tyler Moore had sent the Chief Constable a DVD of his execution which most officers had now seen and even the most hardened amongst them couldn't help but show their emotions. It brought home just how vulnerable they could sometimes be in the process of trying to protect the public from the twisted ambitions of a killer. Tyler Moore had paid the ultimate price, after giving himself to an undercover operation. And he was only twenty-one which made his death even more untimely. The Chief Constable had been in contact with Tyler

Moore's family and told them that their son would be given full police honours at his funeral. A memorial fund had been set up covering the entire Greater Manchester force and it was already in the thousands.

"Do you think we need to get a psychological profiler in here, sir?" Rebecca suggested in a soft voice after watching the DVD. The images of Tyler Moore's horrific death would stay in her head for a very long time. "They might be able to help us work out just who we might be up against here?"

"I think we can work that out for ourselves, DI Stockton," said Jeff who himself was emotionally numb after having watched the video twice now. He had nothing against psychological profilers and had used them in the past but he didn't think it was necessary in this instance, at least not yet anyway. They might have to bring one in later if they haven't made any progress. "I still hold with the idea that this is someone with a grudge of some kind against the Gorton Boys. But I also think he has a grudge against the police because we haven't done what he thinks we should've done in relation to the Gorton Boys."

"John Squires, sir?" Ollie suggested. "Evelyn Squires' son?"

"Well, he certainly feels we haven't got the Gorton Boys under the kind of control he thinks we should have," said Jeff.

"But could he be capable of something like this?" asked Rebecca. "You've met him, sir. What do you think?"

"It's hard to tell, DI Stockton," said Jeff, who wasn't feeling entirely well disposed towards Rebecca at the moment. "But I suspect there's something in his background that we might need to know about so let's start with him. Ollie? I want you to look into his background. Start digging and keep on until something comes up."

"Sir, now that we know that Tyler Moore was undercover, has that brought up any more information on Melanie Patterson that could be useful to us?" asked Rebecca.

"Yes, it has," Jeff answered and handed Rebecca a file that had been given to him by DCI Mike Phillips. "Have a read of that, DI Stockton. I think you'll find it gives you a lot more meat to chew on than before. Has a search warrant been issued with regard to Melanie Patterson's house?"

"Yes, sir," said Ollie. "It's ready and waiting just like the team of officers who are going to swoop on the remaining members of the Gorton Boys and bring them in. They're downstairs waiting for your briefing, sir."

"Good," said Jeff. "Thanks, Ollie. Come down with me and fill in any details I might miss. Read that file carefully, DI Stockton. The press conference I've just done was a decidedly uncomfortable affair. I want some results here to shut them up if for no other reason."

Annabel was nervous at work that morning. Tim was due to take over from her on the afternoon shift after his days off and she'd been texting him for the last couple of days since her little excursion following him but he hadn't replied. Had he seen her checking up on him? It would have been easy down that lonely country lane where the man in the sports car had taken him. If he had, was he mad at her? She wouldn't blame him if he was but she didn't want to lose his friendship or for him to think that she was some kind of crazy stalker. She'd never done that sort of thing before.

"I well wanted a little girl really,"

The last bloody thing Annabel needed was to be doing her shift with one of the summer seasonal recruits who was called Janette. She was only twenty and, although Annabel sometimes found her okay, there were other moments when she found her vacuous, shallow, immature and just plain boring. She was pregnant but hadn't told the hotel before she started so that she'd be entitled to the full maternity package. An example, Annabel thought, of women taking the piss out of the laws that were meant to make them equal and now she was disappointed that she was having a boy instead of a girl.

But she also had a problem with the whole reason why Janette was pregnant. By her own admission, she hadn't even asked her good-looking but hapless boyfriend if he wanted to become a father at the age of twenty. Janette had just decided. Annabel wondered why she wanted to saddle herself with dirty nappies and sleepless nights when she could be out partying and enjoying herself? Why had she made that choice when she was paid peanuts at the hotel and her boyfriend was already doing two jobs to keep a roof over their heads? Annabel wouldn't have missed having Kyle for the world. He was the best thing that had ever happened to her. But, if she was honest, he came along way before her ex-husband Clive was ready to be a father and Annabel had decided that two should become three without having talked to Clive about it. She shook her head in disbelief at the way so many girls these days decide to get pregnant at the earliest opportunity. She wanted to scream at them. They had so many choices and yet they chose to act like they had no choice.

The hotel manager Marilyn Kent walked up to reception with an apparent smile on her face. Annabel thought she must have run over a puppy on the way to work.

"Good morning, Marilyn," Annabel greeted, just to make the effort. Being good at customer service meant you could put on a big smile and a happy face even when you wanted to call the person you were talking to a complete bitch. That's how she was with Marilyn, who was dressed in her usual striped trouser suit and low-cut top that was struggling to accommodate her heaving bosom. High heels completed the ensemble and she, of course, was carrying her radio so that she could be reached quickly if need be. Annabel rarely saw her actually talking into it. She thought it was more for effect than anything else.

"Good morning each," Marilyn responded.

Annabel and Janette might've expected Marilyn to tell them something useful to do with their contracts now that the new owners, who still hadn't revealed themselves, had taken over. But no. She instead treated them to a five-minute description of the row she'd had with her husband the previous evening and about how, if her marriage suddenly ended, she wouldn't ever be interested in seeing other men. Annabel smiled at the way reptiles like Marilyn try to use personal experiences to make you think they were human like you but the fact remained that they were still reptiles.

"I don't suppose you're much interested after your experience with Clive?" Marilyn asked Annabel. "It must've made you wary at the very least."

Annabel was proud of herself that she hadn't let her personal experience with her ex-husband Clive make her all bitter and twisted against the entire male gender. But she'd never been like that. Just because her stepfather had been distant and remote from her all the way through her childhood didn't mean that she could take that out on all men. The same applied to her own weak-willed father who was completely unable to build an emotional bridge with her. And, even though she'd never been unfaithful to Clive and had been devastated when she'd found out that he'd been unfaithful to her, she would still take a risk of being happy with someone else if someone else came along. Just because she was seeing her lover Dermot for sex and friendship didn't mean to say that she wasn't open to a single man coming along and sweeping her off her feet.

"Not really, no," said Annabel. "I don't think you should let one bad experience with one man affect your whole experience with men in the future. They're not all like the one who did you wrong."

"No, I suppose not, and that's a very intelligent way of looking at it," said Marilyn.

"I don't think I've ever been accused of being intelligent before," said Annabel, laughing.

"Well, make the most of it," said Marilyn.

"Have you heard from Tim in the last couple of days, Marilyn?" Annabel asked as casually as she could.

"No? Should I have done?"

It was well known around the hotel that Tim wasn't in favour with Marilyn. It was because he'd challenged the way she ran the place. Not in a particularly confrontational way, but by making suggestions about changes to some working practices that would be more efficient and by speaking out when he didn't think someone was being treated fairly. But Marilyn was one of those managers who was forever saying that she wanted people to use their initiative and that she was always open to suggestions but when people did either of those things she tended to slap them down. Annabel thought that Tim could probably run this place without any bother. He'd once confessed to having many years of managerial experience in a rare moment of candid disclosure. Marilyn had probably seen that herself which was another reason why she'd turned against him. She couldn't have some receptionist making it look like he knew more than she did.

"I just wondered, that was all," said Annabel, lightly. "I haven't been able to get hold of him for the last couple of days."

"Well, he's in for a surprise when he comes for his afternoon shift later," said Marilyn. "As are you all. The hotel's new owners will be revealing themselves to us in a staff meeting at three o'clock. I'll be sending round an email when I get back to my office. Exciting isn't it?"

Both Annabel and Janette stood there wondering why on earth she hadn't told them that when she'd first walked up to the desk instead of boring them rigid with all the shit about the row with her husband. So they were all finally going to know who the new owners were. That would be a surprise for Tim when he came in later.

Bt the time Rebecca and Ollie went back into the interview room they'd been told that another of the Gorton Boys had gone missing. His name was Aidan Richards and he was seventeen. However they weren't planning to question Melanie Patterson about that. They now had information from Tyler Moore's intelligence work that would lead to her detention on charges of conspiracy to murder and living off immoral earnings but some of it still needed to be backed up and they were running out of time before they had to either charge her or release her. Melanie Patterson wasn't waiting patiently. She immediately turned her fire on Ollie after they'd sat down and switched on the interview tape.

"You're an absolute disgrace," she spat. "Sitting there, joining in the oppression of your own black people."

"You mean to say that because I'm an officer in the law enforcement agency of this country that somehow I'm turning my back on my race? You've got a pretty warped vision of what that all means, Mrs Patterson."

"You see," she sneered. "You're even talking like a white man now. You've been lost, brainwashed, taken over. I don't know why I'm even talking to you."

"Well, that's easy," said Rebecca. "You're here talking to us because we're police officers and you've been required to."

"And let me point something else out to you, Mrs Patterson," said Ollie. "You attack me with the bogus and downright insulting claim that I've betrayed my race by becoming a police officer and yet you're here because we believe you've been taking the law into your own hands and getting away with it."

"I beg your pardon?"

"Well, let's make it clear for you," said Rebecca, who delighted in seeing that Melanie looked like she was nervous all of a sudden. She was also relishing the chance to wrong foot Melanie with what she knew from Tyler Moore's undercover work. "Melanie Patterson, you are the power behind the Gorton Boys, aren't you?"

Melanie laughed. "To believe in fairy tales at your age is so desperate and sad."

"Oh, I have the facts to back it up, Mel."

"I am Mrs Patterson to you."

"Okay, Mrs Patterson," said Rebecca. "Then let me spell it out for you because you're in serious trouble."

"I don't think so."

"I know so," said Rebecca, who wanted desperately to wipe that self-satisfied grin off Melanie Patterson's face. It really was getting under her skin. "Alan Chaplin and Reggie Clayton?"

Melanie sighed wearily. "Not them again. I told you I don't know anything about them."

"But you're lying, Mrs Patterson."

"I told you before that I want my lawyer!"

"You ordered the murders of Alan Chaplin and Reggie Clayton. They'd gone against you. You wanted to use them to set an example."

"Oh, carry on with your nonsense," said Melanie, "It's your breath you're wasting not mine."

Rebecca consulted her notes before continuing. "It was about eight o'clock on the evening of 28th August last. You instructed your son Leroy to pick up Chaplin and Clayton and make them believe they were going on a normal raid to deal with someone who wouldn't behave themselves. When they picked you up on the way, the boys didn't even question why you were going with them. You drove them to a piece of waste ground on the other side of Salford where several other members of the Gorton Boys were waiting. It was dark. The nearest houses were too far away for anybody to be able to see what was happening but when Chaplin and Clayton realised they were the targets of that evening's operation they tried to escape. They were stopped and you instructed your son Leroy and one of the other boys to break their legs so they couldn't try and run again. They were in agony but you then gave the order for a car tyre to be placed round each of their necks. You accused them of talking to the police about your activities. They were screaming as they protested their innocence but you were having none of it. You gave the nod and the tyres were doused in petrol and set alight. You watched them die, Melanie. Two young boys who were barely out of school. You gave the order for them to be murdered and you watched as their bodies burned."

"Prove it."

"Then there's the question of the thousands of pounds you hold in an offshore account," said Ollie. "More money than I or my colleague have ever seen in our lives. You have an accountant, someone with a somewhat questionable list of clients, who has made sure that you don't pay any tax on your immoral earnings."

"And where do you think an ordinary woman like me has got that kind of money from?"

"There's nothing ordinary about you, Mrs Patterson," Ollie went on. "Not unless you somehow count forcing drug addicts to prostitute themselves so you make even more money out of them as something an ordinary woman like you would do."

"Have you found my son's killer yet?"

"That is an ongoing investigation, Mrs Patterson."

"Liar."

"Excuse me?"

"You have no intention of finding my Leroy's killer."

"I can assure you we are making every effort to do so, Mrs Patterson."

"Classic tactics of the white-run police force to try and turn the tables on a grief-stricken black woman," said Melanie, bitterly. "But you won't win. The odd battle here and there to play to the white gallery but the war will be won by us eventually because we have justice on our side."

"You can try and talk round it all you like, Mrs Patterson," said Rebecca. "But we have dates, places, names. We also now have statements from other members of the Gorton Boys who've been talking to us. They confirmed all the information we already had and indeed, they've gone further. It's funny how people start talking if they think it can help them get out of trouble."

Melanie leaned forward, purposefully, across the desk. "They wouldn't betray me!"

"Oh, but they would, and they have," said Rebecca, who couldn't help a smirk. "Like I said, they thought they could help themselves by dropping you right in it."

"I'll deal with them."

"And how will you do that? With necklaces? Just like Chaplin and Clayton?"

"Nice try but you'll never get any confession out of me."

"I don't think we'll need one," said Rebecca. "We have enough in the way of evidence, statements and witnesses to events. It's over, Mrs Patterson. Your reign of terror, in which you used the Gorton Boys to carry out your unlawful deeds, is over. Once you're behind bars then the people on the Gorton estate will be able to sleep easy for the first time in years. You've tried to pull the wool over our eyes. You tried to make out to Detective Superintendent Jeff Barton that you were a respectable woman grieving over the loss of her son and blaming the police for not having apprehended the killer yet. But you and I both know that it was all an act designed to throw us off the scent. Well, it didn't work, Mrs Patterson. All it did was lead to you being discovered in all your unlawful glory."

"Where did you get all this so-called evidence from?"

"We had someone on the inside."

"What?"

"Your nephew, Jackson Williams? You won't have heard because it's all happened whilst you've been in here talking to us. He's alive and well and living in America after being adopted by a family in Philadelphia when he was five years old. The young man you knew as your nephew was, in fact, an undercover police officer who gathered up a lot of very useful information for us."

Melanie knew she was trapped now. She'd confided everything to Jackson, especially after Leroy had been murdered. She started to cry.

"My son is barely cold in his grave after being murdered in horrific circumstances and you hit me with all of this and then top it all by telling me the young man who I thought was my nephew come back to me was one of yours? You sick excuse for a human being."

"I recommend you find yourself a lawyer, Mrs Patterson, and fast. I'm afraid this is not going to end well for you."

Jeff and DCI Mike Phillips had been watching from the other side of the two way mirror.

"She's impressive, that DI Stockton," said Phillips. "I've heard she wants to leave your squad, sir? Why is that?"

Jeff paused and then said "She has personal reasons."

Monica went round on her regular visit to dress the ulcers on Ralph's leg and she found him in a pretty agitated state.

"What's wrong, Ralph?" she asked. She was kneeling down and unpeeling the old dressing from the affected area just above his ankle. He was usually full of chat and had a jovial nature which was why she looked forward to her visits. Some of the 'oldies' on her list were like the walking dead. It wasn't necessarily their fault and she did feel awful for thinking it but Ralph liked to make an effort to stay vibrant and aware. Too aware when it came to the activities of the Gorton Boys.

"Why are you asking?"

"Because you don't seem like your normal self."

"That's because I'm not."

"Well then, tell me what's wrong? I might be able to help you."

"It's the death of that young policeman who was working on the estate."

"Oh, I know. That was awful," Monica agreed. "I read all about it in the paper. But don't upset yourself about it, Ralph."

"You don't understand," said Ralph. "I saw him."

"Who?"

"Well, it must've been the murderer," Ralph went on. "I saw him dump the poor lad's body across the road. He was in the same car as before. Why haven't the police responded to my letter? They need to know what I know."

STORMS NINE

Sending that police officer in undercover had been a master stroke. He would concede that. In fact, he would congratulate the police for showing some initiative that otherwise was seriously lacking from the pathetic, empty spaces they called brains. How sweet it was that the police officer in question had fallen into his hands. That would really send a message to them. One day, when all of this comes out, they will realise the consequences of not taking action when they should do. It will make them wake up to themselves and their failings. That's what he hoped anyway.

He opened the door into the chamber. He could hear his latest victim shaking with fear. He could smell the urine that had dried into the floor. Fear always makes them piss themselves and he was well used to having to work around it. He could hear the poor misguided creature struggling against his restraints. They always do that too even though it is pointless.

Aidan was upright and his arms were bent and raised so that his hands were level with the top of his head. His wrists and ankles were cuffed tightly to the structure that he sensed surrounded him. . He also had a belt round his waist that seemed to be attached to something close. He was naked and tape had been placed over his eyes and mouth. He wanted his mum. He wanted his dad. He wanted his annoying little sister. He wanted to be back with his crew, working their streets on the estate. He knew he wouldn't get out of here alive. But how would he die? He knew the horrors that the other two had been through. He'd read in the papers how Leroy and that traitor police officer they'd all known as Jackson had gone. He cried. What the hell did this maniac have in store for his leaving party?

"Hello Aidan," said the man as if he was just greeting him on the street. That's how it had happened. The man had asked for directions and, before he knew it, he was out cold and then the next thing he was here. "Not very comfortable in there is it? But then you see it isn't meant to be. It's meant to be very uncomfortable. It's meant to make you reflect on why you ended up in here. Do you know why you ended up in here, Aidan? Could you hazard a guess at all? Could you maybe pinpoint a time when a certain young girl needed your help? And what did you do? You did nothing, Aidan. You did absolutely nothing. A vulnerable young girl like that and you'll have to go to your maker and explain to Him why you didn't save her. Think you'll be able to manage that, Aidan? Think you'll be able to explain yourself without appearing like a stupid jabbering idiot? If you think that I and what I'm planning to do to you is terrifying, wait until He sends you down to the fires of Hell. That's when your nightmare will really begin and it'll go on for eternity. Your torment will last, literally, for ever. Are you religious, Aidan? Do you get a kick out of the word of the good book? But enough of all these questions. I can tell they'll be tiring for a tiny little brain like yours. But before I leave you to what I know will be a sleepless night, I'll just explain what fun I'm going to have with you tomorrow. Ever heard of an Iron Maiden, Aidan? No? Well, then let me explain. Imagine an upright coffin made of … yes, you guessed it, iron. Well, all over the inside are small daggers. I say 'small' but they're mightily sharp and could cut through silk if need be. Anyway, I digress. The daggers are all connected to each other and, when I switch on the mechanism at the back, they all start to move forward. The apparatus is designed very cleverly so that it pulls each dagger back then shoots it forward, pulls it back and then shoots it forward again. It keeps on doing that until the daggers that will come from behind and to each side of you have met in the middle. The only thing is you'll be slap bang in the middle so, of course, they will have to just stab their way through your body. It will take a minute or two before you reach the point of death and, during that time, you'll be in absolute agony from all the stab wounds. Think about it. I'll be back in the morning."

He started to make his way out of the room and could hear Aidan struggling once more against his restraints.

"It won't do you any good, Aidan. You may as well just not bother, my friend."

The man went back in the next morning. Aidan tried to struggle some more but it was no good. This white man monster knew exactly what he was doing when he'd restrained him. The last few hours had been like Hell. There was no way he could've even tried to sleep. He was so terrified. This was it now. This was the moment. He'd never been religious but now all Aidan wanted to see was his grandma who'd died a few years ago. He hoped she'd be waiting for him whenever he got to whatever 'the other side' was.

"I'll be filming your execution, Aidan and sending a DVD of it to your parents," said the man. "I'm sure they'll always remember the look of sheer terror on your face. Now, before you go, I need to show you that I do have a decent side so I'm going to take the tape from around your mouth and let you have a few last words. But don't yell for help or call out in any way. Nobody out here will hear you anyway."

The man then pulled the tape from Aidan's mouth and as soon as he did Aidan began pleading for his life.

"You don't understand, man, I never did anything to no girl and, whatever I did do, it was all because of Melanie Patterson. She gave all the orders and we just had to follow otherwise we'd go the same way as Alan Chaplin and Reggie Clayton. She's bad news, man, she'll do anything to hold on to what she sees as her power. Please man, I never did anything …"

"Oh, don't start weeping like a stupid little baby," the man ordered sharply. "And don't tell me lies, Aidan. You said you didn't do anything to any girl but that's not true is it? You should've known, Aidan. You should've known after I'd come for Leroy and then the fake Jackson, you should've known that you might be next. I was just wanting to fill you all with fear until I did come for the next one." Aidan started to cry again and the man lost patience. "Oh, shut up!" He placed the tape back across Aidan's mouth and then said. "Did you ever see the film 'Silence of the Lambs'? I loved that scene when Lecter has his victim who he's about to execute and he offers him the choice of being either embowelled or disembowelled. Know that scene, Aidan? Well, I'm going to make you star in your own version of it."

With leather gloves on his hands, the man lifted Aidan's cock and balls and chopped into them with one of the kitchen knives. Blood spurted out all over the place and, with a couple more stabs, they were separated from the rest of Aidan's body.

"Goodbye Aidan. I hope you find what you're looking for in the next life."

The man then switched on the mechanism and the daggers began stabbing their way towards Aidan's body. His death followed shortly afterwards.

STORMS TEN

The atmosphere amongst all the staff at the hotel had improved considerably since the new owners had revealed themselves and made it clear that the only job losses would be amongst the managerial staff. And that meant that Marliyn Kent was told to clear her desk by the close of business that day. What had made her departure even sweeter for all of them was that, when she was receiving a dressing down from the new caretaker manager, he left the intercom on in her office which meant that all working areas of the hotel could hear what he said.

"You have absolutely no idea about managing people, no idea at all. You say your door is always open but you close it as soon as any trouble might be brewing. You keep telling the staff to use their initiative and yet, when they do, you don't like them coming up with a good idea because you hadn't thought of it first. If there are any staff problems, you never want to know about them, even though you have a responsibility, through the duty of care, to sort out any hard feelings that rise up between staff members or, if they have a grievance against you, their employer. I have been through many companies in my career and I have never known a management so incompetent and so ill-equipped to handle people in a customer service environment. You really do abuse the privilege of being useless. You're only interested in the title and not the responsibilities to your staff that go with it and, let's face it, you only got the job because you gave blow jobs to a member of the board of the previous owners. That's probably how you've always had to get your promotions. I'll give you a reference but it will reflect what I see and not the superficial colours you'd like me to paint you as being."

Annabel was laughing so much she almost spat her champagne out.

"I can't believe you said all that," she said, wiping her eyes with the back of her hand. "You got the entire staff on your side in one fell swoop but tell me, why did you hide who you really were all this time?"

"I had my reasons," Tim answered. "I didn't mean to deceive you, Annabel. After all, we've become good friends these past few weeks. But it's the way I operate. I buy the company and then go to work there in a very junior role so that I can see things from the shop floor, as it were. Sitting in meetings with managerial types is all very well and has its purpose but sometimes it gets very tedious and so boring. So I prefer doing it my way and then I get a more truthful understanding of what's going on."

"Like on one of those anonymous millionaire programmes on TV?"

Tim smiled. "You could put it like that, yes. Anyway, what do you think of my real house? But I forgot, you've already seen it even though it was in the dark at the time you followed me out here."

Annabel blushed. "I'm sorry, Tim."

"It's alright, I understand, truly I do. The way I do things does make me seem a little mysterious and you wanted to protect yourself and Kyle. I get that."

Annabel was sitting next to Tim on a large sofa in the living room of his 'real' house along the secluded private road on the outskirts of Blackpool. The room was enormous with floor-to-ceiling windows that opened onto the immaculately kept grounds. Round the other side was a covered swimming pool although the roof could be rolled back in good weather. He clearly believed in minimalism because there was absolutely no sign of the kind of clutter there was in Annabel's house. He looked more relaxed than usual in a plain white open-necked shirt and a pair of black jeans.

"It's important to look after family," said Tim as he stood up and walked over to where he kept drinks in a very modern-looking glass cabinet. He poured himself a scotch. A very large one and placed a couple of blocks of ice in it. "Sorry but I get a bit bored with champagne."

"I've never had that luxury."

"Sorry, I didn't mean … "

"Oh give over. I know you didn't. The reality of your life is different to mine, that's all."

"Clive really wiped you out. I mean both emotionally and financially."

"You could say that," said Annabel. "I kind of resent the fact that he's starting over again and, if he's successful this time, then someone else will share the rewards of that whilst I'm still paying off his debts."

"How did you even begin to get over his betrayal?"

"Well, when you have a son to take care of, then you haven't got a choice but to get on with it," said Annabel who felt that sadness creeping up inside her. She'd always miss Clive. They'd had some bloody good times before it all went sour and she'd always think of him as the love of her life. "Do you look after your family, Tim?"

"No," said Tim. "They wouldn't let me."

"Why ever not?"

"My father died in a massive fire at our house when I was fifteen. We lived on a big farm back then and my mother and my brother blame me for the fire and they've never forgiven me for what happened to Dad."

"But that's rather unfair. It wasn't your fault. Was it?"

"My father and I were having a furious argument, it doesn't matter what it was about, but we had this big oil heater. I knocked it over as I was running out of the house. We had wooden floors, wooden beams, wooden doors. It caught in a matter of seconds and my father was trapped. He didn't stand a chance."

"Oh, Tim," said Annabel. "It must've been hard all these years knowing that your family blame you for what was an accident."

"Yes, it has been," said Tim, who still hadn't sat back down. "What made it worse is that my mother and my brother knew my father was beating me at the time. I came out of the house black and blue with blood pouring from gashes to my eye and to my face."

"Jesus, Tim. Did he always beat you?"

"Yes," said Tim. "Not so much my brother who was big and tough and the kind of son my father wanted. But I was the bookish one. I liked films and I wasn't into my father's chosen sport of rugby. I preferred tennis. He said that he had to beat what he called the femininity out of me and make me a real man."

"What a load of old rubbish."

"Exactly."

"But what was your mother doing whilst all this was going on? Didn't she try and stop him?"

"No. She just stood by and let it all happen," Tim recalled. "She never did anything to challenge my father."

"Did he hit her too?"

"Yes he did. But she always defended him. I became the bad guy for even suggesting she should do something about it."

"You must've had a miserable time of it."

"Well, my childhood wasn't the best, shall we say."

"My Kyle is exactly like you describe yourself at fifteen," said Annabel who'd been touched by Tim's story. She'd never even smacked her son when he was little, she didn't agree with smacking children, and credit where it's due, her ex-husband Clive never touched Kyle either. "I'm glad he's going to grow up to be a sensitive, caring human being rather than a brute who can only talk with his fists."

"You're right he's exactly like I was," Tim agreed enthusiastically. "That's why he and I get on so well."

"You've certainly taken more interest in Kyle than his own father has in recent weeks,"

"That bad, eh?"

"Oh, yeah," said Annabel. "It was Kyle's birthday last Sunday. Clive said he'd be round to take Kyle out and spend the day with him. Kyle was really looking forward to it. He loves his dad. Anyway, Clive rang about ten o'clock and said he couldn't make it after all because something had come up. Kyle was devastated. He ran out of the house saying he hated his life and everybody in it. About an hour later he came back. He fell into my arms, in floods of tears. He said he'd seen his dad going into a pub on Bispham Road with his girlfriend. He said that Clive saw him and then looked away. I haven't spoken to Clive since but when I do he's going to get it, believe me."

"Parents just don't know how much they screw up their children with their crass stupidity," said Tim who meant that more than he could convey. "They just don't see it."

"Tim, I have to ask you," said Annabel. "How did you make your money? I mean, to be able to take over the group that owns the Carrington must mean that you've got something behind you."

Tim turned back to the drinks cabinet and filled his glass with scotch once again. "My maternal grandparents gave me some money. They'd always known what was going on at home and after my mother threw me out after the fire that killed my dad, they took me in and supported me until I was able to stand on my own two feet. They didn't judge me in any way. Then they gave me the money and I invested it. I invested it wisely as it happened. One thing led to another and I became known as a venture capitalist. I've bought dozens of companies, invested in them, put them on the right road to further success and then sold them on at a profit. It's what I do."

"And is that what you'll do with the hotel?"

"Eventually," said Tim. "Not yet."

Tim wanted a cigarette. He knew that Annabel didn't smoke but he thought 'bugger it'. He was in his own home and he wanted one. So he lit one and let the smoke coil into a round shape like it often did when the air was still. It brought about one of those moments between people that Tim had avoided all his life.

"Annabel, you're a very attractive woman and …."

"Oh Christ, I've just made a complete fool of myself."

"No you haven't," said Tim, softly reassuring her. "It's just that … well I can't love anyone. Not in the way that you and most people need."

"Why not? If you think I'm after you for your money then think again because I was attracted to you before I knew about all of this."

"I know, I know, and I don't think it's about my money," said Tim. "It's just that when I try and love someone it always goes wrong. I can't impose that side of myself on you or anybody else, Annabel. You have to believe that it's not you personally that's the problem."

"Are you gay, Tim?"

"I'm complicated," said Tim. "A psychiatrist would have their work cut out if they tried to work me out in that respect. It all goes back to my father and that fire."

"But you can't let that stop you from finding personal happiness."

"Annabel, Annabel," said Tim as he took both her hands in his own. "I can't be that for you. But I have paid off all your debts. Well,, I know they were all Clive's debts really."

Annabel was shocked. "What? They run into thousands. It's going to take me years to pay them off."

"It isn't now," said Tim, happily. "I've paid them off."

"But you can't."

"Well, I have," said Tim. "You'll be getting no more nasty letters and phone calls. You can start again on your own terms."

Annabel couldn't get over it. She was debt-free thanks to this wonderful yet mysterious man. It was like a miracle. A massive weight had been lifted off her shoulders. She and Kyle could start living again.

"I don't want to be paid back," said Tim. "It's a gift. I don't need the money but you do and, even though I can't get emotionally involved with you, I can still be your friend."

Annabel threw her arms round him and kissed him. "Thank you. Thank you so much."

"Do you think Kyle will be pleased?"

"Oh, I know he will. You're already a bit of a hero in his eyes."

"Where is he tonight, by the way?"

"On a sleepover at his mate's house."

"Why don't I take him on Saturday night?"

"Sorry?"

"Well, I know the girls at work are arranging a night out," said Tim. "Why don't you go with them? Kyle can come over here and stay over."

"Really?"

"Why not? I'm not doing anything and I like having him around."

"He'd certainly love this place with the pool and the games room and everything."

"Then it's a deal?"

"Well, I'll put it to him but I can't imagine he'll say no."

"Good that's settled then," said Tim. "And by the way, as you know, I've let the two duty managers from the hotel go. Would you like to fill one of the positions? It'll mean quite a step up in salary of course."

Annabel was crying. "I don't know what to say. In the space of a few minutes you've changed my life completely. I tell you, your family are missing out on a lot if they don't want you in their lives."

"Well, that's a matter you'd have to take up with them," said Tim.

"Just one more thing, Tim."

"Yeah?"

"Who was the guy who dropped you off at the hotel and picked you up outside your little flat that I now know was only for cover?"

"Oh, you mean Joe?"

"If that's his name. I had thought that you and he were an item."

Tim laughed. If only it was that simple. "No, we're not an item. He works for me. He looks after the house, drives me round, runs errands for me and all that. He basically looks after everything so that I can get on with running my business. He's divorced, single, about the same age as you, ex-Army so he's very fit. And he's in the kitchen making dinner for us. Like me to introduce you?"

"After that kind of build up, you'd better lead the way."

Jeff was leaning over a spare desk in the squad room and when he straightened himself back up he launched into the latest briefing.

"Melanie Patterson has been charged with multiple crimes and it will take a lot of work to nail down the details," he said. "But we have managed to crack the whole Gorton Boys gang operation, albeit with a great loss to the force itself in PC Tyler Moore. So the celebrations are tinged with sadness at our loss.

"Leaving that part of it aside for a minute though, sir," said Rebecca. "How the hell did Melanie Patterson get bail?"

Jeff sighed and scratched the back of his head. "The judge decided that, because of the recent loss of her son, it would be inappropriate to hold her in custody," he said. 'I know, it's unbelievable. The nature of her crimes should've kept her detained."

"Her removal does leave us with a relatively clear way as far as the rest of the investigation is concerned though, sir," said Rebecca.

"You're forgetting the murder of her son, DI Stockton."

"I'm not, sir. I'm just saying that, even though we couldn't prove conclusively that she was behind the mob that prevented the ambulance carrying Evelyn Squires from getting to the hospital, we have been able to get her on ordering the looting of Evelyn Squires' house. That means we can concentrate fully on the murders including that of Leroy Patterson."

"And now we might have to add Aidan Matthews to the list making it three," said Jeff.

Ollie Wright then took a call from the desk sergeant downstairs.

"Sir." Ollie began. "There's someone downstairs by the name of Ralph Johnson who says he has vital information with regard to the death of the police officer. He's an old guy apparently and he wants to speak to the officer in charge."

"Okay," said Jeff. "We're due a break so you never know. DI Stockton? You take over from here whilst DS Wright and I go down to speak to this Ralph Johnson. And don't forget the descriptions we've received of the man driving a white delivery van who was seen loitering around the estate before both the second and third abductions. Jeff and Ollie got down to the interview room and introduced themselves to Ralph who was sipping a cup of tea that the desk sergeant had got for him. He'd had to take two buses to get there and walk about half a mile. He was done in and his leg ulcers were really playing him up.

"Are you alright, Mr Johnson?" asked Ollie. The old man was all dressed up in a collar and tie but he looked pale. He made a mental note to arrange for a car to drive him home once they were done. "Is there anything else we can get you?"

"No, son, you're okay," said Ralph. "Have you had my letter?"

"What letter might that be, Mr Johnson?" asked Jeff.

"The one that tells you all I know about the murders of these young lads," said Ralph. "Clearly you haven't but, you see, from my flat on the other side of Manchester Road I can see right into the estate and sometimes it's more entertaining than watching the telly." He took a piece of carefully-folded paper from the inside pocket of his jacket. "So I'll have to start again but first I'll give you this. It's the registration number of the white van that drove onto the estate a few nights ago. I saw the driver get out and dump the body of your officer who'd been working undercover before driving off again at some considerable speed. I saw it all,gentlemen. I saw it all."

STORMS ELEVEN

Kyle and Tim were in the swimming pool at Tim's house. They'd done several lengths and were now taking a breather. They were at the shallow end and were floating about with just their heads above the water.

"I'm going to have a house like this one day," Kyle declared.

"That's the spirit, Kyle," said Tim.

"Thank you so much for asking me over,"

"You're welcome," said Tim. "It'll be something to tell your friends about at school on Monday,"

"I don't really have many friends, to tell you the truth."

"Really? So why do you think that is then?"

"I just don't find many of them that interesting," said Kyle. "They're always doing stupid things and getting into trouble for acting like kids. I've always preferred the company of older people. I get on better with them."

"You are quite mature for your age, Kyle."

"And that's a good thing?"

"Oh, yeah, it wasn't a criticism," Tim assured. If only this young man knew just how beautiful he was. There wasn't a blemish on that perfect skin. No sign of any teenage acne. He was tall, slim. He wore his Speedos well. One of Tim's favourite books was 'Death in Venice' in which the protagonist was a middle-aged man who falls for a teenage boy who's staying in the same hotel in Venice. He saw the love that he felt as something pure and beautiful. He didn't see anything dirty about it and he certainly didn't think of himself as a paedophile. He was a man who'd fallen in love with a thing of beauty. It wasn't his fault that the rest of the world didn't see it that way.

"I don't see myself as settling down with someone my own age either," Kyle went on. "It'll be someone older I think. I think I need a guiding hand and someone who'll lead me through life. I need someone to be the one in charge if you see what I mean."

"I do."

"Have you never met anyone you wanted to settle down with?"

"You ask very candid questions, Kyle."

"Sorry," said Kyle who didn't want to spoil the amazing time he was having by being indiscreet. "I'm a bit like that."

"I don't mind at all," said Tim. "I'm an open book to you, my friend. There was somebody a long time ago. It didn't work out."

"Why not?"

"They died," said Tim. "In a fire that also killed my father. I'll tell you about it all at some point."

"I wish my father was dead," said Kyle, his voice full of bitterness and hurt. He hadn't heard anything from his father since he let him down on his birthday. Today was supposed to be part of Kyle's weekend visit to his father but he hadn't contacted Kyle to make any arrangements. Kyle had tried to keep on loving his father but now he just felt really let down as all his efforts had been for nothing because his father didn't care. And he'd watched his mum worrying herself sick about money and where she was going to get some extra from and that was all due to his father and the hole he'd left her in. He hated his father. He did wish he was dead.

"You don't really wish that, Kyle."

"I do!" Kyle insisted. "When he left us he left my mum in a right mess with money. She told me you'd paid off all her debts. She can't believe how generous you've been to her."

"Your mum is my friend, Kyle. I was able to help, so I did."

"I wish you were my dad."

"Kyle, I could never take the place of your dad and I'm sure that, one day, you and he will be friends again," said Tim. "But I would like to be your friend and help you in whatever way I can."

"I think that would be cool."

"Good," said Tim, who was becoming overwhelmed by that familiar feeling he'd experienced so many times before. It was risky and it was dangerous because nobody else understood. But it had now begun to unfurl and, even if he wanted to, he couldn't stop it now. "Now I think we'll be good for a few more lengths."

"I bet I can beat you."

"Now that gives me a challenge, young man. Okay, on your marks, get set, go!"

Tim had given his assistant Joe the night off and so he made dinner for himself and Kyle. Annabel had told him that steak and chips was Kyle's favourite meal so that's what he'd cooked for him.

"I can really talk to you, you know," said Kyle as they sat at the table after finishing their food. They were both in T-shirts and jogging pants. It was loose. It was relaxed. He felt close to Tim. Closer than he'd ever felt to anyone before. He was tall and handsome like his dad. And yet he wasn't his dad. He was cultured, educated, successful. In truth he was everything his dad wasn't.

"I'm glad about that."

"I can talk to you about really deep stuff," said Kyle. "My Mum, God bless her, doesn't have a clue about what I'm going on about half the time. Neither has my dad. I love my mum, don't get me wrong, I love her to bits, but I can't talk to her like I can to you."

"We're just different people, Kyle, that's all," said Tim. "Look, it's getting late. Why don't we change into our pyjamas and lounge in front of the TV? I've put some pyjamas out for you on your bed."

When they were both changed, Tim into his shorts, T-shirt and bathrobe and Kyle into his striped pyjamas, they re-assembled on one of the sofas. Tim put the TV on. '*Match of the Day*' had just started which seemed to please Kyle.

"Ace," said Kyle. "By the way, these pyjamas seem really old. The colours on the stripes have all faded."

"That's because they are old and yet they fit you perfectly," said Tim who was being taken back in time by the sight of Kyle in those pyjamas. "Come and join me on the sofa. The night, as they say, is still young."

"Look, do you mind telling me what I'm doing here?" asked John Squires. He was sitting in the interview room and had just been joined by Jeff and Rebecca. "You do know I recently buried my mother and can do without any hassle just now?"

"Yes, we're aware of all that, Mr Squires," said Jeff, who had just been informed that the body of a young black man had been found dumped on the edge of the Gorton estate. He had multiple stab wounds and, although no formal identification had taken place, it was believed to be Aidan Matthews "But I'm afraid something's come up that we need to talk to you about urgently."

"Go ahead," said Squires. "I've got nothing to hide."

"Are you sure about that, Mr Squires?" asked Rebecca.

"What do you mean by that?"

"Mr Squires, do you own a white Transit van with the registration number PX54 GRU?"

"No, I don't. Next question."

"I'm going to give you another chance to answer that question, Mr Squires," said Jeff.

"You can ask me as many times as you like, Superintendent, it won't change the answer," said Squires. "I don't own a vehicle like you describe."

"Then why is it registered to you at your address?" Jeff pursued. John Squires seemed as belligerent that day as when he'd first come across him in his mother, Evelyn Squires', house. He was one of those men who still believed that Britain had an empire and ruled the waves with a mixture of colonialism and exploitation. He was the sort that Daily Mail leader writers dream of. No departure from the old ways. No questioning of the assertion that whichever way the British do it, is the best and the only way. No doubt of the belief that the rest of the world should bend to the

British way and not the other way round. Jeff felt sorry for him and those like him. They were living in the dark ages. They were holding the rest of the country back from making real progress in the 21st century.

"Mr Squires, the van that's registered in your name, and with your address, was seen being driven onto the estate. Our witness says he saw the driver, a man of your build, get out and dump the body, the decapitated body, of PC Tyler Moore on the pavement before driving off at speed."

"This has got absolutely nothing to do with me."

"Then can you tell us what you were doing last Tuesday evening around ten o'clock?"

"I was at home with my wife and we were watching television."

"And is it only your wife who can confirm that?"

"Yes!"

"Keep calm, Mr Squires."

"Keep calm? You tell me to keep bloody calm when I'm in here having to answer for a most heinous crime that I had nothing to do with?"

Jeff and Ollie stayed silent. They both watched the facial expressions of Squires as he tried to work out what to say next. Whenever a suspect was brought into the station in connection with the killing of a police officer, it always put everyone on edge. Both Jeff and Ollie knew that their colleagues would be lining up to 'sort Squires out' for what he'd done to PC Tyler Moore and they would all have heard of the DVD the killer sent of Moore's execution. They had to get to a tangible result soon.

"Look, I know what's going on here," Squires sneered, his eyes beginning to show the full vent of his anger. "This is all your politically-correct bullshit. A proud white woman who was dedicated to her race is murdered by a heartless mob and you don't give a damn. Not really. But as soon as one of the black thugs is picked off, then all hell breaks loose in trying to get to his killer. And then one of your own, an actual serving black police officer, is done in and you're tripping over yourselves to pick on innocent victims like me."

"Victims of what, Mr Squires?"

"Victims of the political correctness that says you must find the killer of blacks before whites in case you're accused of racial discrimination! Do I have to spell it out to you? Well, I'll tell you what political correctness is. It's verbal fascism, that's what it is. It's telling me I can't say what I like in my own country."

"You were born in what was then Rhodesia, Mr Squires?" said Jeff, who'd decided to let Squires get all the ranting he liked out of his system. It only made him look worse. He was giving them more motive with each racist utterance.

"Of British parents!"

"Did you have a good relationship with your parents?" Ollie asked.

"What the hell has that got to do with it?"

"I'm just asking."

"None of your damn business but, yes, I did have an excellent relationship with my parents "

Jeff and Ollie decided to take a break from the interview and consulted Chief Superintendent Geraldine Chambers in the next room where she'd been watching the interview by way of the two-way mirror.

"The man certainly has principles but they're not the kind I share," said Geraldine, shaking her head slightly. "So gentlemen, what are your initial thoughts?"

"My instinct jury is still out, ma'am," said Jeff.

"Mine too, ma'am," said Ollie. "I'm the first to condemn racism but a racist isn't necessarily a killer. However, I would like to question him on other aspects of his life,…. like why he frequents the 'Hare and Hound' pub in Stockport."

"Isn't that the pub that's under investigation over the suspicion that the far-right Albion Movement meets there?"

"Correct, ma'am," Jeff confirmed. "It was fairly active in the northwest a few years ago and everyone thought it was all but gone. But now it seems it's coming to life again."

"Okay, well keep going," said Geraldine. "We've got to get to a result on this one, Jeff."

"We're doing our best, ma'am,"

Jeff and Ollie went back into the interview room where Squires was sitting with his head in his hands.

"Do you like to have a few pints down the pub of an evening, Mr Squires?" Ollie asked.

Squires raised his head sharply and said "I suppose you're going to tell me that's a bloody crime now?"

"Not at all," said Ollie. "But it's where you drink and who you drink with that matters to us."

"Police fucking state or what?"

"Do you drink at the 'Hare and Hound' in Stockport?"

Squires paused. It was the first time they'd seen a chink in his armour of certainty, the first time he'd seemed knocked off balance by a question.

"Yes, I go to the 'Hare and Hound'," Squires confirmed without looking at Ollie.

"It's about five miles away from your house in Cheadle," said Ollie. "Aren't there pubs nearer to where you live that you could go to?"

"What can I say? I like the beer at the 'Hare and Hound'."

"Do you attend meetings of the Albion Movement there?"

Squires' face contorted in a mixture of cynicism and pure contempt. "I'm aware that there are members of the Albion Movement who meet there and I may drink and discuss stuff with them, yes."

"Do you or do you not attend meetings of the Albion Movement at the 'Hare and Hound' pub in Stockport Mr Squires, yes or no?"

"Yes, I attend those meetings! I detest what all this multicultural bullshit is doing to this great and once proud country."

"Once proud?"

"Well, we can't be proud of it anymore," Squires asserted. "Not with all the mosques and the Muslims running riot all over the bloody place. And its time all the blacks got to know who's the bloody boss in this country. I'm not ashamed for being associated with a movement that believes in restoring the natural supremacy of the white, Christian race in Britain."

"So you're an apartheid movement?"

"I can't think of a better word for it, yes."

"White people living in the good parts of town whilst blacks and other racial minorities are placed in camps that stretch for miles and condemn all living there to poverty."

"You're painting a mightily pretty picture to me, young man."

"Restoring the natural order?"

"That's it."

"So what would you do with a black like me who's just as proud to be British as you are but who's a serving police officer?"

"Well, you wouldn't be able to carry on as a police officer," said Squires, smirking. "But we'd find you a job cleaning the floors and the toilets. That would be more where you fit into the natural order of things."

Jeff was impressed with the way Ollie was keeping his cool under intense provocation. But he also knew there were limits. He could see from Ollie's face that there was a rage going on inside. Not surprising with all the offensive shit coming out of Squires' mouth and pelted like stones in Ollie's direction. There was an anger in Squires too. That was very clear. The kind of anger that could drive him to murder? Whoever had killed Leroy Patterson, Tyler Moore, and Aidan Matthews had done so with meticulous planning. That needed cool, calm reflection rather than angry outbursts of potentially uncontrollable anger.

"What did you do with them, Mr Squires?" Jeff asked.

"What do you mean?"

"The murders of Leroy Patterson, Tyler Moore, and Aidan Matthews would've required a lot of thought and application. How did you manage it? Where did you take them? Where did you get the apparatus you used to murder them?"

John Squires threw his head back and laughed. "You're making a big mistake here, Superintendent."

"Are we?" Ollie asked. "You've made very clear your distaste for black people, Mr Squires."

"Don't you try and twist my words, boy ... "

"It's Detective Sergeant Oliver Wright to you, Mr Squires."

"Get the job so that the politically correct quotas looked good?"

"Now that's enough, Squires," Jeff interrupted. "You've been asked some serious questions because we believe you're in serious trouble. As we speak, a team of officers is searching your home. Your white Transit van is nowhere to be seen and isn't even parked nearby. So why don't you save us all a lot of time and tell us what you've done with the van and how you came to commit these murders?"

"If you upset my wife in the course of your ridiculous and useless search of my house then I will deal with whoever is responsible."

"Like you dealt with the three members of the Gorton Boys who ended up dead?" asked Ollie. "Or is it only black people you have murderous thoughts about?"

"You're treading on thin ice, boy."

"The van seen that night was registered to you, Mr Squires," Ollie went on, ignoring having been addressed so disparagingly again. So why don't you stop playing games that are not that clever and start co-operating? It will be to your benefit in the end."

Annabel had found Tim's assistant, Joe, to be rather engaging. True he was fit and good looking. You'd notice, in a good way, if he walked in the room. And he made her laugh too. But she detected a rather large chip on his shoulder where women were concerned. Like with many people who appear to be happy on the outside, you only have to scratch the surface a little to find the potential demons lurking inside. A lot of people put on an act. They show the world a face that betrays the real one underneath. She'd done it herself at times. It was almost like a defence mechanism.

But it was when the subject of previous relationships came up that the chip controlled by the demon came up. Suddenly he didn't seem to like the fact that she was divorced with a teenage son to bring up. He also questioned her account of how her marriage had failed. He said it was unfair of her to put all the blame for the collapse of her marriage on her husband and that she must've done something to him to make him walk out, leaving her with piles and piles of debts.

"It didn't go well, then?" said Tim who was talking to Annabel in the office that went with her new role of hotel duty manager. "And before I left the two of you to it, you seemed to be getting on great."

"Well, we were," said Annabel. "Until I told him about Clive."

"Joe was left pretty bitter by his divorce," Tim explained. "His wife had an affair but she ended up throwing him out for some reason. Then she made it very difficult for him to see his daughter, who he hasn't seen now for years, and he's been back and forth to court I don't know how many times. I know that it's all hit him hard."

"Well, I'm sorry about all that but we're all different," said Annabel, who was trying to keep her married lover Dermot at bay for the moment. He'd started telling her that he was developing feelings for her and she didn't know if she really wanted that. She'd never really thought about it because she thought they were just having fun. He'd even mentioned leaving his wife and she didn't know if she wanted that either. She wasn't one of those daft girls who have affairs with men who are already attached and then get all moralistic and hypocritical when he mentions leaving his current partner because the girl having the affair doesn't want to be seen to be breaking up somebody else's relationship. What did they think they were doing when they started sleeping with him? They want to have their fun in private but be seen to be a 'really nice person' to the outside world. No, she wasn't like any of that duplicitous lot. But she didn't know if she cared enough for Dermot to want him to leave his clearly unhappy home for her. She wouldn't have minded stepping out with Joe for a while and seeing how things went. But it didn't look like she was going to get the chance. He hadn't even asked for her phone number.

"But we're all different, Tim," Annabel asserted. "And we've all been through different situations. I don't blame all men for the way Clive treated me and he shouldn't treat all women as if they're the same as his ex-wife."

"I understand that," said Tim, who was glad she hadn't brought up the subject he thought she might have done. "But Joe is not in that same place. I don't know if he ever will be."

"Before you go, there's something else I wanted to talk to you about," said Annabel.

Tim was suddenly nervous. He'd just taken control of one of the leading hotel chains in the north but he suspected that the question that was about to come would reduce him to jelly deep down inside. "Oh, yeah?"

"What did you do with Kyle at the weekend?"

"Sorry?"

"Well, since he came back from your place he's been wandering round moodily. He's been up and full of the joys of Spring one minute and then apparently down in the depths of despair the next. You wouldn't know anything about what might be driving that?"

"No," said Tim. "Why would I?"

"Well, I thought he might've confided in you and sometimes, when you do that, situations that weren't real before suddenly become very real to you," said Annabel. "And he's constantly sending and receiving messages on his mobile phone. I mean, if I didn't know any better, the way he's acting would make me think he'd fallen in love or something."

STORMS TWELVE

It was the way Tim had looked at Annabel when she said that if she didn't know any better she'd think that Kyle was falling in love by the way he was acting. It made her suspicious. Tim was a highly successful businessman who was loaded. Regardless of his sexual leanings, he should have been spoken for when you consider that and the fact that he isn't exactly ugly.

It was all starting to fall into place now and she didn't like the picture it was painting. Tim had seemed particularly enthusiastic about getting to know Kyle and about having him over to stay. She hadn't wanted to believe anything as gross as what was playing out in her mind now. But maybe she'd been such a bloody fool. She'd had her suspicions about Tim right from the start because of how he seemed to want to hide himself away. She understood why when it came to taking over the business. But now she had to face the fact that her son had fallen into the trap of a sexual manipulator. And she'd let it happen.

She sat in the kitchen staring at Kyle's mobile phone. She'd never looked at it before. She'd never had cause to. It was one of those lines you don't cross with teenagers. Or maybe she'd got that all wrong. Maybe she was the most useless mother in the history of useless mothers. No, she didn't think that. She was a good mother to Kyle. She'd just made a serious error of judgment where Tim was concerned and now she couldn't forgive herself.

Kyle was upstairs in the shower. She knew it was a total invasion of his privacy but did she really have any choice? Ever since he'd come back from his weekend stay with Tim, he'd had his mobile virtually strapped to him and he'd been on it almost constantly. Was it Tim he was exchanging messages with? Had he met someone else whilst he was there? She was going out of her mind and, in the end, she just grabbed it and pressed the message key.

And then she got all the proof she needed and it made her feel sick to her stomach.

From Tim: *Saturday night was sensational. You've turned a light on inside me.*

From Kyle: *I can't believe all those things we did. You're like a magician.*

From Tim: *You feel good then?*

From Kyle: *I feel absolutely fucking fantastic!*

From Tim: *I told you I'd make you feel that way.*

From Kyle: *And you weren't kidding.*

From Tim: *We have to keep it to ourselves though, my dear Kyle. Nobody else must know, especially not your mum because they wouldn't understand.*

From Kyle: *No, I know and I understand. But when will I see you again?*

From Tim: *Can you invent a sleepover at one of your mates?*

From Kyle: *Yeah, that should be easy enough. Mum won't suspect anything.*

From Tim: *You're her angel child.*

From Kyle: *I felt more like a devil in your arms.*

From Tim: *I've been walking around ten feet off the ground.*

From Kyle: *Me too. I didn't think it was possible for me to feel like this. Thank you.*

From Tim: *We'll just have to keep it quiet until you're sixteen. Then we can be open about it.*

There were many more messages along the same lines but Annabel had read enough. She couldn't help, though, looking at two video messages but immediately wished she hadn't. The first one was from Kyle and was a full-frontal nude of himself. The second one was from Tim. He was masturbating to the nude picture of Kyle. She ran over to the kitchen sink and threw up. She retched deep inside her stomach and brought back everything she'd consumed that day. She wiped her mouth and then looked up as she heard Kyle come into the room.

"What's the matter, Mum?" Kyle asked. He was dressed in his dark blue bathrobe and was drying his hair with a towel as he walked towards her. "Are you okay?"

Annabel could feel the colour draining from her face. "We need to talk, Kyle."

"This sounds serious," said Kyle who then noticed his mobile phone was still in her hand. "That's my phone,"

"I needed to know what you'd been doing, Kyle."

Kyle grabbed his phone from her. "You read my messages? They're private!"

"Kyle, I'm not angry with you," said Annabel. "But you must understand that what you've been doing with Tim is wrong."

"Why is it? It makes me happy."

"But you're too young, Kyle," Annabel pleaded. "Son, it isn't your fault."

"It isn't Tim's fault either."

"He took advantage of you."

"I wanted to be taken advantage of! Don't you see? I wanted this as much as he did!"

"But he's the adult and he should've resisted."

"Like you should've resisted when you started shagging the married hotel handyman?"

Annabel slapped his face. The look on his face said it all. Wrong move.

"Oh, Kyle, I'm sorry, I'm so sorry, I shouldn't have done that."

"No, you shouldn't. Because it's made me more determined than ever to carry on with Tim."

"No you can't because you're underage and I absolutely forbid it!"

"See if I care what you think."

"Kyle, he's breaking the law."

"Then it's a stupid law if it stops people loving each other."

"But you're only fifteen and he's forty-three. It is all absolutely wrong and I'm going to put a stop to it."

"Mum, if you make trouble for Tim over this then I promise you I'll take off from here and you'll never see me again."

Annabel could feel tears running down her cheeks. "Kyle, what the hell has happened to you? I could never imagine you'd speak to me like that."

Kyle started to feel guilty. He loved his mum. He always had done. It was his dad he despised and really didn't want to upset his mum. She'd been there for him all the way. She always had been. But now he felt like he was kicking her in the teeth.

"I'm sorry, Mum. Okay? I'm sorry if I've hurt you. But this thing with Tim has made me feel so much better about myself and about life. It's lifted me right up there and I just don't want to come back down."

"But you have to, son," said Annabel. "And I'd be failing you as your mother if I didn't take steps to put a stop to all this."

Kyle started to cry. Annabel tried to comfort him but he pushed her away.

"You do that, Mum. You do that and I will hate you for the rest of my life!"

Kyle ran out of the kitchen and up the stairs. Annabel was crying herself now but there was only one person who could help her. He always said he'd be there if ever she needed anything.

Well, she'd never been more in need of help than now and so maybe it was time to see just how good his word was.

Ollie Wright pinned the pictures of the three murder victims on the whiteboard in front of the entire squad. First Leroy Patterson, then PC Tyler Moore and finally Aidan Richards.   He then put up a picture of John Squires, who remained the chief suspect. Chief Superintendent Geraldine Chambers was also in attendance.

"Thanks, Ollie," said Jeff, stepping forward. "John Squires is an angry man. He's also an unapologetic racist. As you all know. his mother. Evelyn Squires. was prevented from getting to hospital by a mob from the Gorton estate that prevented the ambulance she was in from moving. She died as a result. He had every motive to carry out a vendetta campaign against the Gorton Boys gang and I've always said that this was something personal. This is something aimed, fair and square, at the Gorton Boys because they've done something that's ripped the heart out of the killer in some way. And I suspect it was something that we, the police, either couldn't do anything about for some reason or wouldn't do anything about. I've spoken to DCI Mike Phillips who was the senior officer who placed PC Tyler Moore into the undercover operation as Melanie Patterson's nephew Jackson Williams. As far as he's concerned. there was no crime that his team overlooked in order to protect PC Moore's identity. Then there's the matter of the white Transit van that was seen by Ralph Johnson who lives in a flat on the second floor of Wavertree Gardens over the road from the main route into the Gorton estate. His front room window gives him a clear view of the entrance into the estate and he's written down many of the comings and goings of the last few weeks. He's been trying to get in touch with us for a while apparently. He saw the van drive into the estate last Tuesday night and watched the driver get out and dump Tyler Moore's body. He didn't get a close look at the driver but he's coming in this afternoon to view some pictures that will include John Squires."

"What if Mr Johnson doesn't positively identify John Squires as the man he saw last Tuesday night?" asked Chief Superintendent Chambers. "Where would that leave us?"

"Ma'am, John Squires has the motive."

"But?"

"Where did he take them? Where did he get hold of the gruesome equipment he used to kill them? These are questions he will have to answer if Ralph Johnson positively identifies him but, if Johnson doesn't, then we'll keep going back to the basic questions until we find a way to the end of this."

Rebecca smiled as she led Ralph Johnson through the station. He was clearly enjoying the attention and why should she bother about that. The old bloke was probably as lonely and hadn't had any real attention for months, maybe even years. He had told her that he had two daughters and a stack of grandchildren, none of whom he saw on a regular basis. That was the trouble with families these days, thought Rebecca. Nobody seems to give a shit. He said he'd put his best clothes on but he still had that smell of an old person who'd given up taking any real care of himself. He was lovely though. She'd really quite taken to him.

"I've got a nurse who looks a bit like you," said Ralph.

"Oh, yeah?" said Rebecca.

"Her name is Monica and she comes to dress the ulcers on my leg twice every week," Ralph announced proudly. "She's a good sort although I don't think she posted the letter I'd written to the police."

"Why do you think she didn't do that, Ralph?"

"Well, she said she was worried I might get into bother with that Gorton Boys gang and whoever was doing them in," Ralph explained. "She thought I should just lead a quiet life and not get myself involved with anything."

"She was only looking out for you," said Rebecca.

"But I could have given you that registration number long before I did and you could have been working on it sooner."

"Oh, well," said Rebecca. "You were trying to do the right thing. What's Monica's surname by the way?"

"Her surname?"

"Yes. Just as a matter of interest."

"Well, it's Parkinson. Yes, that's it. Monica Parkinson. She works out of the surgery on Palatine Road."

"Oh, yes I know that place," said Rebecca. "My Aunt Shirley goes there."

"Is she pretty?"

"Behave," said Rebecca. "Yes, she is pretty but she's been well spoken for to my Uncle Dennis for nearly forty years."

"Pity."

"You're incorrigible,"

Ralph chuckled. "Well, I'm sure I am, if I knew what that meant."

Jeff and Rebecca set Ralph up in a more comfortable room than the standard ones they used for interviews and showed him several pictures of known criminals who might have had reason to want to 'score' against the Gorton Boys. It was when they got to the pictures of John Squires that their interest in Ralph's answers really picked up.

"Was this the man you saw driving the Transit van, Ralph?" Jeff asked.

"No," said Ralph. "As I said to you before, I didn't get a good look at him but I do remember his build as being more stocky than that. And he was shorter too. This man here is too tall to be the man I saw."

Jeff got home that night in time to read Toby a bedtime story before tucking him in for the night. He always tried to get home in time for this and felt guilty when he couldn't. After Toby's mum died, Jeff had made every effort to be there for his son whenever he needed him. But it wasn't always easy with the job that he had.

"Goodnight, soldier," said Jeff, who then kissed his son. "How many weeks now to your sixth birthday?"

"Twenty-two, Daddy!"

"Only twenty-two? That still leaves me lots of time to plan our little trip to Disneyland."

"I can't wait."

"Me neither, mate. Now, before you go to sleep, is there anything you want to talk to me about?"

"I don't think so, Daddy. Everything's cool really."

Jeff smiled. "I'm glad about that, mate. Now have a good night's sleep and I'll see you in the morning for breakfast."

Jeff then went downstairs and poured himself a glass of red wine from a bottle he'd already opened. He then asked Brendan, his live-in nanny and housekeeper, if he'd like one too. Jeff didn't think of Brendan as just an employee. He'd become part of the family.

"That would be great thanks, Jeff," said Brendan who was warming up Jeff's dinner of lamb casserole with a selection of roasted vegetables.

"That smells wonderful," said Jeff, who wasn't very hungry but didn't want to tell Brendan that after he'd gone to all this trouble. Ralph Johnson declaring that John Squires was not the man who'd been driving the white Transit van had proved a blow to the whole case. Chief Superintendent Chambers was getting edgy. The higher reaches of the force and the press were both on her back. It was Jeff's job to produce a result that she could then go to all the hungry wolves with. They'd have to get their heads together again in the morning. Somewhere, in all the stuff they already knew, there was something for them to go on.

"Well, I hope you've got an appetite because I made plenty," said Brendan. "But, no pressure, I can freeze what you don't eat."

Brendan sat talking with Jeff at the table whilst Jeff ate. Something about the flavours in the casserole ignited Jeff's appetite and he managed to eat most of what Brendan had dished up for him without feeling like it was a chore. Jeff had to smile. They were a right pair of sad fuckers sat round the dining table like an old married couple. Jeff knew that Brendan wanted to find himself a boyfriend but couldn't seem to find the right guy and Jeff himself had reached the stage of grief where he was ready to smell a woman on his sheets again. But it wasn't as simple as that. He'd have to go through the whole dating thing before any of that happened.

Jeff was just about to open another bottle of wine for them to share when the doorbell rang. He sighed heavily.

"Do you want me to get that?" asked Brendan, who was already making for the door.

"Would you mind? Whoever it is can get to bloody fuck. I'm not in the mood tonight."

A few seconds later, when Jeff had opened the second bottle of wine and poured a glass each for himself and Brendan, he felt the draught come through the house from the front door still being open. Brendan then reappeared in the dining room.

"Who is it?" Jeff asked.

"Jeff, there's a woman here with her teenage son. She says she's your sister, Annabel, and the boy is your nephew, Kyle."

Ralph was feeling very pleased with himself that he'd made some sort of a contribution to a police investigation. It had raised his spirits no end and he couldn't help boasting about his experiences to Monica when she came round with his new set of tablets to control his blood pressure. He didn't even notice at first how cross the news was making Monica.

"What did you tell them, Ralph?" she asked.

"I told them everything I knew. They were very impressed."

"What was it exactly that you told them, Ralph?" Monica demanded in a sharp voice.

"I gave them the registration number of the white Transit van and … anyway, what's it to you what I told them?"

"You gave them what?" she asked, as she stepped forward towards him.

"What the hell has got into you? You're making me nervous."

"You couldn't help yourself, could you?" she sneered. "You've got such a sad fucking excuse for a life that you couldn't help meddling in things that don't concern you. Don't you understand? Are you too thick to see? I didn't post your stupid letter to the police because I didn't want you to get involved. But now you've left me no choice, Ralph."

"What are you talking about? Get out! Go on, get out and send me a different nurse."

Those were the last words spoken by Ralph Johnson before nurse Monica Parkinson punched him in the face and carried on punching and kicking the old man until she was sure that he was dead.

STORMS THIRTEEN

Jeff was driving Annabel up the M61 to Blackpool. Kyle had stayed at Jeff's house in the care of Jeff's brother Lewis.

"I'm really sorry for dropping all this on you, Jeff," said Annabel.

"Nonsense," said Jeff who almost felt like he was playing truant. He'd rung Rebecca and Ollie to say he would be taking some time this morning to see to a personal matter. The timing was beyond lousy and he really should be leaving it to his Lancashire CID colleagues. But this was personal. This was family. He shouldn't be investigating but he had to at least start the process of sorting it all out even if it wasn't entirely professional. "You're my sister, Annabel."

"Half-sister," said Annabel. "Same dad, different mum, remember?"

"I don't keep it in mind, Annabel."

"I'll bet your mum does," said Annabel. "I'll bet she wished I'd never come along."

"Well, I suppose you are a reminder to her that dad had an affair that you were the result of," said Jeff. "But I wouldn't know for sure. I don't speak to mum and dad, Annabel. As you know, they didn't even come to Lillie Mae's funeral. Neither did my other sister who's supposedly full blood and yet takes the same racist line as my parents. You came. Our Lewis came. You two are the ones I think of as family."

"I'm sorry I've not been in touch lately, Jeff."

"We've all had a lot on."

"That's no excuse," said Annabel. "I then drop on you when I've got a crisis. What does that say about me as a sister?"

"Don't beat yourself up, Annabel."

"But it's true," she insisted. "I've been a lousy sister and now I've been a lousy mother too."

"That's not true," Jeff insisted, firmly. "What happened to Kyle is not your fault."

"But I'm his mother. I should've protected him."

"But you heard the way he spoke last night. Annabel, I've interviewed hundreds of people in my time as a police officer. It doesn't sound as if Kyle was an entirely unwilling participant in the activities with Tim Ryder. But what happened was wrong, it was unlawful and Tim Ryder should've been protecting Kyle from Tim Ryder. I understand that teenagers these days are a lot more sexual than even we were at that age and I've heard psychologists argue that it is somewhat ridiculous to assume that, just because someone becomes sixteen, they're more sexually responsible for themselves than they were a year before. Some teenagers do develop earlier than others in that way. But the law is the law, Annabel, and it's there for a reason, to protect the vulnerable and to protect childhood. Tim Ryder broke it and I don't care how rich he is or how influential he is, he has to pay, simple as that."

"Thank you, Jeff," said Ananbel.

"What for/"

"For being there for me," said Annabel. "For being a true and very good brother."

Jeff followed Annabel's directions and, in broad daylight, it was relatively easy to find the house because it stood out as the biggest amongst some very big pads. Jeff said it was one of those places where you could almost smell the money in the air.

"I'm nervous," said Annabel. "I feel physically sick."

"Don't be," said Jeff. "You're not the one in the wrong."

Jeff drove up to the gates. Annabel got out of the car and walked round to the driver's side to press the buzzer. She thought it wouldn't arouse Tim's suspicions if it was her voice he heard. After she'd waited a few seconds, she pressed it again and when Tim answered she simply said "It's Annabel."

The gates opened and Jeff drove them through and down the short drive to the house.

"He's certainly done well for himself," Jeff remarked.

"Better than he should have done," said Annabel. "I'm getting angry now, Jeff. I'm getting very bloody angry."

"Good," said Jeff. "Anger is the right emotion here. All that guilt you were feeling before was misplaced."

They passed a large garage to the side of the house. The door was about halfway open but it was enough for Jeff to be able to see the registration number of what looked like a white Transit van. It was PX54 GRU. For crying out loud! It was the van that had been seen by Ralph Johnson on the Gorton estate when the driver dumped Tyler Moore's body and which is registered to John Squires. So what the hell was it doing here?

"What's the matter?" asked Annabel as Jeff took out his mobile phone and began dialling.

"I'm calling for back up," he said. "I've just seen something that could throw a whole new light on proceedings. Stay in the car and don't move. Your friend Tim may be a lot more dangerous than we thought."

Later that day. Rebecca and Ollie began interviewing Tim Ryder. Jeff and Chief Superintendent Chambers were watching in the usual way through the two-way mirror.

"Your excursion to the seaside may have accidentally led us down the right road," said Geraldine. She was hurting all the way down her left hand side. Her partner Hazel had been particularly desperate last night and Geraldine thought one of her ribs might be broken.. But the painkillers were taking care of it so it can't have been that bad. It was horrible to go through though. She was frustrated with herself that she hadn't done anything about it yet. She was a senior police officer for God's sake. She wasn't the sort who was afraid of spiders or the dark. It was crazy that she let Hazel take out her frustrations on her. She'd like to open up to Jeff. She thought he might be able to understand. He was certainly probably the only one of her professional colleagues she'd trust to tell all to.

"It's just a shame my nephew had to go through what he did in order for the right road to come to me, ma'am."

"Yes, I'm sorry Jeff. That was insensitive of me."

"No it wasn't," Jeff assured. "You were stating a fact, that's all."

Geraldine leaned forward and rested the palms of her hands on the wall.

"Are you alright, ma'am?" Jeff asked.

"Yes," said Geraldine, as brightly as she could manage. "I'm fine, Jeff."

Jeff didn't believe a word of it and made a mental note to question the Chief about it once the case was wound up. She was clearly in pain of some kind.

"I don't expect you to understand," said Tim, in a soft voice that betrayed the fear that was building inside him. It had been a long road that he was just coming to the end of but he knew what they did to men like him in prison. The day of reckoning was near.

"What don't you expect us to understand, Mr Ryder?" Rebecca asked.

"That what happened between me and Kyle … I didn't mean him any harm."

"We have a detailed statement from Kyle Matheson, Mr Ryder," said Rebecca. "A very detailed statement. I'm just wondering what you would want to tell us?"

"I would've remained faithful to him. He's a beautiful boy."

"And how long would that have lasted, Mr Ryder? Until he reached eighteen and therefore a bit too old for your particular taste?"

"You are disgusting," Tim spat. "I'm not the monster you think I am,"

"Mr Ryder," said Rebecca. "The facts are that you are forty-three and Kyle Matheson is fifteen and so, therefore, it is not only wrong for the two of you to engage in sexual activity but it's also against the laws that are there to protect children."

"That's what he said," said Tim.

"Who? Who said what to you?"

"My father. All those years ago he used that as an excuse to beat the shit out of me. Oh, I knew the day would come when I'd have to answer for what I've done. But do you want to know why I'm like this? Do you want to know what happened to make me this way? You think you're so clever, sitting there in judgment on me."

"I think you'd better tell us, Mr Ryder," said Rebecca, feeling like she was about to hear another sob story.

"If you go into my background, you'll know that my father died in a fire when I was a teenager. This was back in Rhodesia, where we had a farm. He was beating me up one night and do you know why? It was because I'd fallen in love with one of the other boys at school. His name was Jonathan and my father caught us together in my bed. There was a terrible scene. I managed to break free of his grip somehow and ran as fast as I could out of the house. I knocked over an oil heater we had, and because there was so much wood in the house, the fire caught straight away and my father was trapped. He died in the fire and my mother and brother disowned me after that. They blamed me entirely for my father's death. I was sent to England where I was taken in by my mother's parents. They'd never liked my mother's choice of husband so this was like power to their cause. I ended up changing my surname to theirs because I didn't want to be reminded of my immediate family's rejection of me. They gave me the money to start a business which is how I became wealthy but, you see, Jonathan also died in that fire. He was trapped too. The pain of knowing that I got out but Jonathan didn't has tortured my soul ever since. You have no idea of what it's put me through. I never wanted to let go of Jonathan. Because I wanted so desperately to go back to the days before we were discovered and because I wanted so badly to somehow bring him back to life, I found I could never love anyone of my own age. They had to be the same age as he was. Do you see? Can you find it in your hearts to see the pain I've been in all these years? I had to try and bring him back to me because I'd never stopped loving him. I'll give you dates and time and names of all the other boys like Kyle. Because of my wealth I was able to pay them all off. That's why I don't have a criminal record. I thought I'd be able to pay Annabel off but it seems she's too principled."

"That's all very touching, Mr Ryder," said Rebecca who had little sympathy for the man sitting opposite her. Childhood traumas were one thing and she understood the kind of deep, long-lasting effect they can have on someone. But surely there comes a point when you have to stop using them as an excuse for the wrong you commit years later? Tim Ryder was an intelligent man so why couldn't he have taken the decision to stop chasing underage boys for sex? He knew it was against the law. He knew it was reckless and potentially damaging to the young boys concerned. So why did he carry on doing it for the sake of a memory, a tragic memory but still only a memory nevertheless. "But the fact remains that you had sex with a minor."

"He consented."

"However much he consented. the onus was still on you to stop it happening."

"As a matter of interest, Mr Ryder?" said Ollie who was going on a feeling that had come to him whilst Ryder had been talking. "What did you change your name from?"

"Squires," Tim answered. "My name before was Tim Squires."

The following morning, as the squad was gathering, the news came through about Ralph Johnson.

"Apparently, his usual nurse didn't turn up for work this morning and they had to send one of the other nurses to make the regular call on him to dress his leg," said Ollie. "She says that the front door was ajar so she went in. She found him on the kitchen floor. He'd been battered to death."

"Have they managed to contact the nurse who didn't show up?" asked Jeff.

"No," said Ollie. "She's not answering either her mobile or her home phone."

"Her name is Monica Parkinson," said Rebecca. "Ralph Johnson told me about her. Remember he said he'd sent us a letter but we never received it? Well, it was her that he gave the letter to for posting. I know it's a big leap but can you see where I'm going with this?"

"But what would she have to do with the Gorton Boys?"

"Who knows, but what's interesting for us here is the fact that her partner is called Joe Briers."

"The same Joe Briers who works for our friend Tim Ryder?" said Rebecca.

"The very same," said Ollie, before picking up his vibrating phone. "As an assistant and housekeeper."

"Well,, well, well," said Jeff. "Why do I feel like the pieces are beginning to come together?"

"Sir, that was the search team at Tim Ryder's house. Downstairs in the basement, they've found a large reinforced metal door that it's taken them some time to get through. But they've just made it and, beyond the door, they found a large, cavernous, room with various items of torture and execution equipment inside, including a garotte, a guillotine and an Iron Maiden."

"So that's where he took them," said Jeff. "But which '*he*' are we talking about? Tim Ryder or Joe Briers? Do we know where Joe Briers is, Ollie?"

"No, sir. He's gone to ground, just like his wife."

Before they were able to return to questioning Tim Ryder, a young heavily pregnant woman turned up at the station. She said her name was Charlotte Briers and she wanted to tell her story to one of the detectives handling the investigation into the killing of members of the Gorton Boys. She looked clean and her clothes well kept, despite her assertion that she'd been sleeping on friends' sofas for nights on end.

"I think it's my dad you're looking for," she said.

"Why do you say that?" asked Jeff.

"Look, I've been in hiding for weeks now," Charlotte announced. "I've been hiding from my dad and from that bitch, Melanie Patterson."

"Why's that?"

"My mum and dad divorced years ago when I was about eight or nine," said Charlotte. "My mum had met someone else and she wanted to go off with him. It was never very fair on my dad but, once he gave her the divorce she wanted, she started turning funny about him seeing me. It was as if she wanted to wipe him out of our lives completely and concentrate on this new man she'd met. I didn't think that was fair on my dad but what could I do? I was just a little kid who cried herself to sleep every night because her mummy told her that her daddy didn't want to see her. But it was all lies. My mum was telling a pack of absolute lies. Anyway it turned out that I didn't see my dad or have any contact with him for years. My mum and me used to argue a lot when I was growing up and I resented her for being so obstructive about me seeing my dad. I hated my stepfather. He was just a flash bastard with a nice car. Anyway, I fell in with the Gorton Boys. Some of them went to my school and I became Leroy Patterson's girlfriend. He was lovely to me. He treated me really well and we really got on. But his mother, Melanie, didn't like it. She didn't like him having a white girlfriend. So she arranged to have me raped."

"What?" Rebecca questioned. "Are you serious?"

"Deadly serious," said Charlotte as she rubbed her stomach. "There was a whole gang of them. That's how I ended up like this."

"So you're pregnant because of having been raped on the order of Melanie Patterson?" said Jeff.

"Yes," said Charlotte who started to cry. "Sorry."

"Don't be," said Rebecca who handed her some tissues. "I think you're being remarkably self-assured."

"I don't always feel it."

"No, I expect not," said Rebecca. "But does your father know about you being pregnant?"

"Yes," said Charlotte. "During one of his many attempts to try and see me, my mother said I'd been taken off by the Gorton Boys and that he should ask them if he wanted to know anything about me. He came down to the Gorton estate. He saw me, because even after the rape, I didn't feel like I had anywhere else to go. I told my dad everything. He wanted to take me home with him but I still had faith in Leroy. Then, after he disappeared and was found to have been murdered, I didn't know what to do. I knew that Melanie Patterson would try and blame me in some way so I ran."

"We'll get you some help, Charlotte," said Jeff. "We will. But tell me, how angry was your dad when you told him what had been happening to you?"

"Very angry," said Charlotte. "He was very angry. I think that he's the murderer you're looking for."

STORMS FOURTEEN

Melanie was beyond feeling terrified. She'd answered the door and had let the man in when he said he had information that could help her fight the charges that had been made against her. The next thing she knew, she was stuck in wherever the hell she was now. She was restrained to some kind of post with her hands cuffed together behind her. She was standing on what felt like some kind of platform and her ankles were strapped together too. Another strap was holding her head up against the post. Her eyes and mouth were covered in tape. It felt cold, wherever she was, like there was a lot of space around her but what she couldn't work out was what her feet were buried in. It felt like straw and it came up to her knees.

She wanted to scream out for help but she couldn't. She was going to die. She knew that. And if it was the same killer who'd got to the three boys, then how in God's name was he going to kill her? She could hear someone shuffling about near to her. It must be him.

And then that voice…….. That cold, menacing voice she'd never heard before.

"Melanie? Are you awake? Of course you are because I can see you struggling against your restraints which. Incidentally. won't do you any good. I know what I'm doing and I do it well. But then you should know that, considering what happened to three of your boys. Ooh sorry, yes, one of them was an undercover police officer who you knew nothing about. That was mighty careless of you, Melanie. He'd have told his bosses everything before I got to him. But that's why you were arrested and charges been made against you, isn't it Melanie? But that's not why you're here. No, you see, you're here because of my daughter. You know her. Her name is Charlotte Briers and she was going out with your son, Leroy. But you didn't like that, did you? You're as racist as any white bigot and, being the sadistic bitch that you are, you ordered for her to be gang raped. Well, I'm her father and I was denied the chance of watching her growing up thanks to another sadistic woman who used to be my wife. I couldn't be there to protect her, even though the courts eventually found in my favour, after years of trying. But then my ex-wife wouldn't comply with the court order giving me access and the court wouldn't enforce their decision. They said they had to think of my ex-wife's distress but what about mine? What about my distress at not being able to see my daughter? Did they ever think of that? No! And then you and your Gorton Boys come along and try and take her away from me just when she was getting to that age when she could make up her own mind about seeing me. She fell in with your boys and the police said they couldn't help me because she was old enough to decide for herself who she sees. And yet, they had one of theirs in there who could've saved her from being raped on your orders. You'll be pleased to know I've saved the best till last, Melanie. Your execution is going to be the most spectacular. You'll burn your way into the next world, Melanie. Death by fire."

Monica Parkinson was apprehended when she tried to get back into her house. She was brought down to the station and interviewed by Jeff and Ollie. She made a full and tearful confession to the murder of Ralph Johnson. She said she liked Ralph and felt sorry for him because his family seemed to have abandoned him but when she knew he'd given details of the van registration number to the police something inside her just snapped because she wanted to protect her partner, Joe. Even though she knew what he'd done, she couldn't let some interfering old man drop Joe right in it.

"How did Joe get hold of a van that was registered to Tim Ryder's brother?" Jeff asked.

"John Squires has a carpet shop in Cheadle," Monica explained, still wiping away the tears. "He's a very proud man and would never admit this to you but trade was bad and he was having severe difficulties with his cash flow. So he came to his brother Tim to see if he'd help him out financially. As part of the deal, Tim bought that van off John and asked my Joe to change all the registration details. But I think Joe saw it as an opportunity to use the van to carry out his plans and, if it was registered to someone else, then it would take the police off the scent."

"And you knew all of this?" Jeff pursued.

"Yes. Tim Ryder confides in Joe about everything. Joe even knew about the affairs Tim had with teenage boys. Well, if you can call them affairs, that is. It was Joe who delivered the pay-offs to all the parents involved so that they wouldn't go the police. Those parents were equally as guilty as Tim, in my opinion, for letting it happen and taking the money."

"And Joe wasn't complicit in the cover-ups by delivering the cash?" Rebecca scoffed. She couldn't stand it when people who were so much in the wrong like Monica tried to claim some moral high ground somewhere. It made her want to slap her.

"Yes, I know," said Monica. "But I was in love with Joe and I'd have done anything for him."

"Did you know that Tim Ryder encouraged a flirtation to take place between Joe and a woman called Annabel Matheson?"

"Oh, he was always doing that," said Monica, dismissively. "It was all part of the games they used to play. Joe is a very good-looking man and he likes to flirt. I don't mind as long as it stays there and doesn't develop into anything else."

"But why didn't Joe go the police about Tim Ryder's affairs with teenage boys when he knew it was all so wrong?"

"Because Tim was paying him a lot of money."

"It's that easy?" said Rebecca.

"Yes, it is," said Monica. "Look, Joe has been through a really hard time over the years with his ex-wife and the constant battle for access to his daughter Charlotte."

"But why didn't you try and stop him from doing what he did?"

"Do you really think I could have stopped him?" Monica pleaded. "Joe was determined. He said he had to speak up for the rights of fathers to protect their children from scum like the Gorton Boys.."

"Where is Joe now?"

"All I know is that he was going after Melanie Patterson. He couldn't believe that she'd got bail but saw it as a golden opportunity to go after her."

Jeff went back upstairs to where several members of his squad were gathered. He was about to check on the progress in the search for the whereabouts and arrest of Joe Briers that was now several hours old when Ollie called him over to his computer.

"Take a look at this, sir," said Ollie.

"Shit," said Jeff. "Direct it to the main screen please, Ollie."

Seconds later the large main screen in the squad room was filled with the image of Melanie Patterson awaiting her execution at the stake on the pyre that Joe Briers had built.

"Where the fuck is that?" said Jeff.

"I'm checking the IP address of the signal now, sir," said Ollie and, moments later, he was able to confirm that it was coming from somewhere on the Gorton estate.

"It looks like some kind of warehouse," said Rebecca.

"Well, there's only one of those on the Gorton estate," said Jeff. "It's disused and right in the middle. Get the team down there now! Rebecca, you go with them and report back to me as soon as you can. I want the fire brigade and an ambulance down there too and impress on them the need for urgency. Ollie, has he set the link up for sound?"

Chief Superintendent Chambers walked into the room just in time to hear Joe Briers answer Jeff's question to Ollie.

"Yes, I can hear you, copper," said Joe. He was looking into the camera from three or four metres back and in his hand was a gas cylinder burner with the flame looking clear and strong. "Can you hear me?"

"Briers, there's a team of officers on their way to you as I speak," said Jeff. "You won't be able to get away with this so why don't you give up now? It's over, Briers. It's over."

"Not quite, policeman. You see, I've got a few things to say. The police have never been my friend. All the years I spent fighting my ex-wife through the courts just because I wanted to be a father to my daughter and none of you lot helped me. All you ever told me to do was to keep calm. '*Mr Briers, don't lose your temper. Mr Briers, it'll only harm your case if you do, Mr Briers.*' My ex-wife could throw all manner of emotional shit around and yet, if I so much as raised my voice with sheer exasperation, I was told it would harm my case. Do you know how that feels? Do you know how it feels to spend years fighting somebody who's taken your relationship with your daughter away from you? Something so basic in life as that? And I wouldn't mind if my ex-wife was a good mother. But she isn't. She's a lousy mother. So bad that she lets my daughter fall in with the Gorton Boys. I'm Charlotte's father. I should've been there to protect her. But it was taken away from me. They raped my daughter, copper. They raped my daughter and I only found out because I went looking for her. I found her. But she told me to go away and leave her alone. She told me I was out of my depth and that I couldn't help her. I told her I'd get them. I told her I'd get them for her and they'd all pay."

"Look, Joe," said Jeff. If he could keep him talking until Rebecca and the Major Incident Team arrived, there might be a chance. But the local uniformed officers should be there by now. He'd be checking the local station's response times after this. "I'm a father. If someone took my relationship with my son away from me, I'd want to kill them. I'd be in a mess, Joe just like you were. I'd probably lose it …."

At that moment, there was a commotion to the left of the picture. Jeff heard the familiar bellowing of officers making their presence felt. 'Police!' He then watched in horror as Joe Briers lit the straw with the gas burner. Within seconds it was all the way round the edges of the mass of straw that circled Melanie Patterson's feet. One of the uniformed officers grabbed Briers who lifted the burner and aimed it in the officer's face. The officer screamed with pain and stumbled as he covered his face with his hands. The other officer, who'd been frantically looking for something to put the fire around Melanie Patterson out, then went for Briers and this time he managed to wrestle the burner out of his hands and get him face down on the floor. He then got the cuffs on him and left him lying on the floor before turning his attention to the fire which was now raging.

"See to your fellow officer first!" Jeff shouted.

And then the screen went black.

"Ollie! What's happening?"

"We've lost the connection, sir."

"Well, get it back!"

"It's no good, sir. Something must've happened at that end,"

"It was one of the biggest fires ever attended by the Greater Manchester Fire Brigade," said Chief Superintendent Chambers in her office. Jeff was with her.

"There were all kinds of flammable materials in that warehouse," said Jeff. "And fire seems to move quicker than water. The sad thing is that four people lost their lives including two uniformed officers at the start of their careers. I don't break my heart over Joe Briers or even Melanie Patterson though. They got what was coming to them."

"I don't think anybody would argue with you about Briers or Patterson," said Geraldine. "A case of natural justice taking its course with regard to those two."

"Briers was an embittered man," said Jeff. "I don't condone what he did but I could understand him. With some people, if they don't feel they're getting the justice they deserve, they let it ride for years and then they explode with frustration. The criminality of Melanie Patterson is one thing but with Briers it goes back to one woman thinking she has the right to stop a father from seeing his daughter, just because she can, and him losing his head because of it. It's wrong, ma'am. It's so very wrong."

"Okay, but getting back to the basics of the case," said Geraldine. "I take it that Briers was able to use the white van without Tim Ryder knowing because Ryder was busy being an anonymous employee at the Blackpool hotel and not actually living at home full-time?"

"Yes, ma'am," said Jeff. "I believe Ryder when he says he was completely unaware of what Briers was up to. The news has devastated him as much as it has everybody else. Briers' daughter is in pieces, which is not a good condition considering she's about to give birth."

"To a child that was conceived in a rape."

"Literally a gang rape, ma'am," said Jeff. "That poor kid has already been through so much. It's going to take a lot for her to move on from all this."

"Is she going to keep the child?"

"She says she is," said Jeff. "I don't know if that's such a good idea but she seems fairly determined."

"She'll get a lot of help, Jeff."

"I know but … well I'd advise her to give the baby up for adoption and then take some time to work out what she wants to do with her life. But I'm just a police officer. I'm not a social worker or a therapist."

"You're a very thoughtful officer who thinks way beyond the crime, Jeff, and I value that although you do realise it wasn't a good idea for you to go chasing up to Blackpool in pursuit of Tim Ryder when your sister was making a complaint against him involving your nephew?"

"I do, ma'am, yes, but Annabel and Kyle are family and I needed to do it that way."

"Just so that you remember, and I'm sure you do, that a good lawyer might make something out of it when it comes to court?"

"I do realise that, ma'am, but I stick by my decision," said Jeff.

"Okay," said Geraldine. "But look, Jeff, I'd like to change the subject completely and talk to you about something else."

"Of course. Is it something personal?"

"How did you guess that?" asked Geraldine who'd decided to tell Jeff about her home situation.

"I think you've got some serious troubles at home. Am I right?"

Before Geraldine could answer they were interrupted by Ollie Wright knocking and then putting his head round the door.

"Excuse me, ma'am, sir but something's happened that I thought you'd want to know about straight away."

"What is it, Ollie?" Jeff asked.

"It's Tim Ryder, sir. He's been found hanged in his cell."

STORMS FIFTEEN

"This is lovely," said Annabel who was sitting with Jeff in his back garden. They were sharing a bottle of Australian Chardonnay.

"It's a shame we haven't done more of it," said Jeff. "But we'll have to make up for lost time."

"We will," said Annabel. "It's also a shame, of course, that it took what happened to Kyle to bring us back together."

"Well, we were never really apart, Annabel."

"No, but you know what I mean. I mean it can't have been easy for any of you to accept me as your sister when I was the result of an affair your father had whilst married to your mother."

"I don't judge that way, Annabel," said Jeff. "Neither does our Lewis. My sister is another matter but then she's so much like my mum and our dad."

"I guess the boys will be back soon," said Annabel.

"I told Lewis I'd be firing up the barbecue about three so I expect them any time soon," said Jeff. His brother Lewis, with his partner Seamus, had taken Jeff's son Toby and Annabel's son

Kyle to play football in the park down the road. Jeff's live-in nanny and housekeeper Brendan was on a day off and had gone to see his parents.

"Lewis and Seamus seen very happy," said Annabel.

"Oh, they are," Jeff confirmed. "Seamus transferred a few months ago to being a pilot on long-haul flights from Heathrow so he spends a bit more time away now than he used to. But it seems to have made their hearts grow fonder for each other."

"I think they're one of the few stable couples in the family."

Jeff laughed. "Yes, I think you're right. How's Kyle coming on, by the way?"

"His therapist is pleased with his progress so far," said Annabel. "He seems to be doing well but you never know."

"You know you could consider suing the estate of Tim Ryder for compensation just like the families of all those other boys are doing," said Jeff.

"No, I'm not going to go down that road, Jeff," said Annabel, who had thought about what Jeff had suggested but felt that she and Kyle had had enough. "He paid all Clive's debts off for me. I'll take that as compensation."

"Fair enough," said Jeff.

"But Jeff, how could he have come to hang himself? Wasn't he being watched in case he tried to do that very thing?"

"Yes he was and there's going to be an enquiry," said Jeff. "But it's not unusual in cases like this. I'm not saying that the prison was complicit but we'll see what the conclusion of the enquiry says."

"I wanted to have my day in court, for Kyle's sake," said Annabel. "I think he needed to see just how wrong Tim had been towards him."

"I know and it frustrates me too," said Jeff. "But look, Annabel, I've been thinking. The case I've just wrapped up had family bitterness right at its heart. Tim Ryder and John Squires were kept apart by a family feud and, if that had not been the case, then perhaps Tim Ryder might have been able to get the kind of professional help that would've stopped him doing what he did. I don't want our family ever to be estranged again, Annabel so I've got an idea to put to you."

Annabel was intrigued. "Go on….."

"You don't want to go back to that job at the hotel so why don't you and Kyle move in here with us for a while until you sort yourselves out with your own place?"

"Wow," said Annabel who was delighted at the invitation. "But have you really thought about this? I mean you've got a tight little unit here. Do you really want us to walk in on it?"

"I wouldn't have asked you if I didn't," said Jeff. "I just think it would be good for us all to live within a larger family unit for a while and really get to know each other."

"Kyle is about to start his final year before his exams though, Jeff."

"I know but he could transfer to a school round here and still complete them, I'm sure. So what do you say?"

"Well, I'll have to put it to Kyle first but if you're sure and he says its okay then yes, why not? We'll make a fresh start after all that's happened and leave recent events behind us. Clive won't mind. He doesn't care enough to mind."

"I've already spoken to Brendan and he says its fine by him and I know Toby will be cool so speak to Kyle when they get back from football and we'll move ahead with it."

They clinked their glasses to celebrate. "Cheers, brother," said Annabel.

"Cheers, little sis."

There was a ring of the doorbell and when Jeff went to answer it he was pleasantly surprised to see Rebecca Stockton standing there. He greeted her warmly and asked if she'd like to join him and Annabel in the back garden for a glass of wine and then stay for the barbecue.

"I'll see," said Rebecca, who hadn't slept all night because of what she'd been planning to do. "But could we talk first?"

"Sure," said Jeff who led her into the living room. They sat down close to each other on the sofa. Jeff was sure he knew what Rebecca had come to talk to him about and perhaps it had been long overdue. "What's on your mind?"

"Jeff, I want to change my mind over the whole transfer request," Rebecca began.

"Okay," said Jeff. "I never wanted it to happen anyway."

"I know. You, me and Ollie Wright are a good team."

"Well, I think so and I certainly don't want to break it up."

"But it's more than that for me, Jeff. Look, I have feelings for you. I have had for a long time and I didn't want to make it too obvious before out of respect for Lillie Mae and the grieving process you've been going through. I get that you never wanted to even consider a relationship with another woman until you'd worked it all out inside. I do get that, Jeff. But I felt that now was the time to tell you and that, if I didn't tell you, I'd regret it."

Jeff stood up and walked over to the window. "It's not that I've never thought about us being more than friends, Becky. I have. But that's just it, I've never thought about it seriously until recently."

"And what conclusion have you drawn, Jeff? I mean, could you ever love me the way I love you? It's taken a lot for me to come here with this and I need to know how you feel about me."

THE END

But Detective Superintendent Jeff Barton and his team will be back in "*No Questions Asked*', .

Here's a preview of Chapter One.

Gary Mitchell was a butcher. He'd inherited his late father's business a few years ago and still kept the sign above the shop that read 'G. Mitchell and Son'. The 'G' stood for George which had been his father's name. He and his wife Debbie had been trying for children for years without any success and, now that they were both in their early forties, the clock was ticking away for Debbie especially so she'd decided to seek IVF treatment. They'd now been on it for a while and still it wasn't producing any results which meant that Debbie was getting more desperate and more obsessive. Gary would've been happy to adopt but Debbie wouldn't hear of it. She had to have her own children and not somebody else's. It was a somewhat irrational disposition coming from a woman who was known for looking at things in an extremely rational way. Whilst Gary had been building up his business, Debbie had gone to university as a mature student and come out with a first class degree in Management. She was now a senior manager with the local NHS Trust and was responsible for strategic planning. She earned a salary that went way beyond what Gary took for himself from the business and they were comfortably off. After twenty years of marriage they knew each other inside out but Gary was certain his wife didn't know about his little visits to Lucy across the road or any of the other times when he hadn't been a saint as far as his marriage was concerned.

"That was magic as always, Lucy Lou," said Gary as he withdrew from inside her and fell onto his back. He was still hard. "Absolutely magic."

Lucy swept her hand across his stomach and through the hairs on his chest. She rested the side of her head on his shoulder and breathed out a sigh of deep satisfaction. He always did it for her. He'd never let her down. If only he could consider her in ways that weren't just to do with sex. He placed his arm across her back and held her to him. She didn't want him to go. She never wanted him to go. But now the deed had been done, she knew that a part of him would be wanting to sneak back across the road to spend the rest of the day in cozy domesticity with the delightful Debbie. Lucy had never liked Debbie. Even without the complication of sleeping with her husband, Lucy thought that Debbie was a pretentious snob who looked down on Lucy because she was a single mum and the only resident of their short street who rented her house instead of being an owner-occupier like the rest of them.

"Have you had your Sunday dinner?" she asked him rather lamely. It just seemed like the right thing to say, for some unfathomable reason.

"No," Gary answered. He thought it was a bit of a strange question but he was used to that with Lucy. She could be an odd one at times. "We're going to Jeff Barton's barbecue later."

"'We?'" thought Lucy. That, of course, means Gary and Debbie. After the way he'd made her feel during their lovemaking, it was like a sudden stab through the heart to hear him say 'we' and know that he wasn't referring to her. Lucy wondered if there would ever come a time in her life when she would come first with a man. She'd always had to content herself with so little when it came to the pursuit of personal happiness. She'd had to hold her head up high despite knowing that none of her lovers had ever felt the same for her as she felt for them. She'd had to watch people leave her with apparent ease. It hadn't seemed to bother them that much. None of them had seemed to care that they were breaking her heart. Of course, they all made the right noises and gestures about how there was someone out there for her and that she was a beautiful girl and it wasn't her, it was them. All the usual bullshit aimed solely at helping them deal with whatever they had that passed for a conscience. She'd given everything to every man there'd ever been in her life and done whatever she could to meet their needs whilst watching them not giving a second thought for whatever she needed.

"OK, right," said Lucy. "I think the whole street is going."

"You are too, then?"

"Yes. But you ask like I shouldn't be going?"

"Well, it … well it might be a bit awkward, that's all."

"Awkward for whom?"

"Lucy, don't take this the wrong way, but you and me standing there, large as life, trying not to look at each other in that way and knowing that we're making a complete fool out of poor old Debbie," said Gary. "It just doesn't seem right or fair."

It never ceased to amaze Lucy how married men who have affairs with other women display a level of insensitivity that is mind blowing. Nobody had ever cared whether or not she'd been made a fool of. But the little wife at home must always have her feelings spared.

"So it's okay for me to sit here all alone after you've gone and eat beans on toast for my Sunday dinner whilst you and your wife enjoy yourself at Jeff's barbecue? It's only across the road, Gary. I'll be able to bloody hear you."

"Won't Bradley be back soon?"

"He won't be back until later," said Lucy, who thanked God for her son Bradley. Without him to be responsible for, she'd probably have topped herself years ago although that didn't stop her from feeling guilty that he'd never had a dad.

"Do you want Debbie to find out?"

"What kind of a question is that?"

"Because that would unleash Hell on me."

Lucy stroked Gary's arm. "Baby, I'm sorry," she pleaded, suddenly afraid that he might call time on their affair as being too much trouble. She always regretted asserting herself in case it led to her losing what precious little she had. And, at the moment, that meant looking forward to Gary coming over a couple of times a week and being hers just for that short time he was there. "I just got a bit carried away. Of course I don't want Debbie to find out. I don't want this to end."

"Good," said Gary. "And look, on second thoughts, there'll be plenty of people there for us to get lost in the crowd. You can go if you want to."

"Only if you're sure it won't make things difficult for you? I mean, I've got plenty to do here like the ironing and stuff."

"I am sure," said Gary. "You deserve to have a good time as much as anybody, Lucy. But best to try and stay away from me as much as you can whilst you're there."

"Okay," said Lucy who wanted to burst into tears but would wait until after he'd gone.

"And, Baby…"

"Yeah?"

"You wouldn't go off with anybody else, would you? Not in front of me. I'd hate to see that."

"You know I wouldn't do that to you," said Lucy.

"I know."

"Would you like a coffee before you go?"

"I've been banned from having coffee," said Gary. "Debbie read somewhere that it can have an adverse affect on a man's fertility and you know how desperate she is to get pregnant."

Lucy wanted to scream. "Tea then?"

"Yeah great and I'd love a biscuit if you've got one. I need to put some energy back in my body after you've been abusing it."

"I'd better bring you up the whole packet then."

"It's nature, not nurture, Annabel," said Jeff, sitting in his back garden with his sister Annabel. "Just because Toby is surrounded by gays doesn't mean to say he'll grow up to be gay himself. I grew up to be straight because that's who I am. Our Lewis grew up to be gay because that's who he is."

"Yeah, I get that," said Annabel who'd been thinking about her son Kyle and his apparent sexuality. "So it wouldn't bother you if Toby grew up to be gay?"

"No, of course it wouldn't," said Jeff. "I'm surprised you're even questioning it."

"Jeff, I didn't mean anything by it. I'm not homophobic. It's just that I didn't expect my fifteen year-old son to have his sexuality awakened by a forty-three year old man."

"Annabel, Tim Ryder was breaking the law."

"Yes, I know, but I thought he was a good man. A man who I thought was my friend."

"So, hang on, is this about you or about Kyle?"

"Jeff, that's not fair!"

"So explain it to me then."

"Tim Ryder was only using me to get to my son. I'm finding that hard, Jeff. I'm finding it hard to think that he was looking at Kyle in that way and that I had led him to Kyle."

Jeff held her hand. "I know you are, sweetheart. But Tim Ryder was a highly devious man and anybody would've fallen under his spell."

"And now the lives of me and my son are full of social workers and therapists. He was examined by a doctor. If Kyle really is gay then I don't have a problem with it. But he's still a child, Jeff. He's my child and I'm scared for him."

"What are you scared about?"

"That Tim Ryder has marked him for life and he won't be able to get above what he did to him to work out who he is," Annabel explained, tearfully. "I'm sorry to keep banging on about this, Jeff."

"No need to apologise," said Jeff reassuringly. "And now that you're moving in here with Kyle, we can talk about it whenever you like. But, right now, I do need to get this barbecue started before everyone starts arriving."

Annabel wiped her face with her fingers and tried to snap out of the decline she'd got into. "What do you want me to do to help?"

"You've already made those wonderful big salads."

"I know but I can do more," said Annabel.

"I tell you what, Gary from two doors down is a butcher and he got me all the meat. He brought it over last night. It's in the fridge on a big tray if you want to get that for me."

"Okay," said Annabel. "By the way, where did Rebecca go?"

"She went to the supermarket to get some more wine," said Jeff. "She'll be back soon."

"She's a very pretty girl, Jeff, and she clearly has eyes for you. So are you going to do anything about it?"

"You don't mess about!"

"Jeff, I can see how lonely you are."

"Well, yeah, I have more or less decided to give it a go with Rebecca."

"More or less?"

"Well, there's always a whole set of unknowns when you go into a new relationship," said Jeff. "So we'll see what happens and take it a day at a time."

"Excellent. I think that's the right decision."

"Except for one thing."

"What's that?"

"I've been holding off from even thinking about seeing another woman because, to do so, would mean I have to stop dreaming about Lillie Mae not being dead."

"Oh, Jeff," said Annabel. She rested her head on his shoulder. "Me and my big mouth. I'm sorry."

"No, no it doesn't matter really."

"I just want you to be happy again."

"I want that too, Annabel, but to get to that point, I have to finally accept that Lillie Mae is gone and won't ever come back," said Jeff, his voice trailing off. "That's what's been hard. I loved the bones of her, Annabel. Nobody had ever made me feel the way she did and, when Toby came along, it was like life was really complete. She was an exceptional wife, an exceptional mother and an exceptional human being. She was way out of my league and I was bloody lucky to have had her even for those few years. I'll never be that lucky again."

"Well, no, it won't be the same with someone else like Rebecca, Jeff," said Annabel. "Rebecca isn't Lillie Mae. But she's got gifts of her own and she could make you happy, if you gave her the chance. You deserve to be happy again, Jeff. Give yourself that chance."

Debbie Mitchell drove her car onto the driveway of her house and stopped for a moment. She'd been to see her brother and sister-in-law who'd just had their third child. He was a bonny little thing and they'd called him Casey. Debbie was going to be a proud aunt who would dote on her nephew like she doted on her other nephews and nieces but she still wouldn't be able to stop it all from breaking her heart. She was so desperate for a child of her own. She had to get pregnant and it wasn't fair that she was still waiting.

She walked in through the front door just as Gary was coming down stairs. He was dressed in his usual check shirt with the long sleeves and the buttoned down collar and a pair of light blue jeans. She'd come to hate the kind of shirt that he was so fond of.

"Aren't you going to put something else on?" she grumbled.

"What's wrong with this?" he asked, as if he didn't know.

"Jeff must've seen you in that old thing a thousand times."

"Debbie, Jeff is a man much like me. I won't take any notice of what he's dressed in and he won't take any notice of what I'm dressed in."

"No, but I do."

"Well, get over it because I'm not changing."

"Have you only just got up?"

"Yes," he answered defensively. "I get up at six every morning except Sunday and if I want a lie-in on a Sunday, then I'll have one." Except that a lie-in had meant nipping across the road to have it in Lucy's bed as soon as Debbie had gone off to her brother's.

"You make me sound like a real nagging wife."

Gary smiled. "You have your moments."

"Hey, I was joking, you cheeky bugger."

"I wasn't."

"Gary! I'm not one of those kind of women."

"You are when it comes to a certain subject," said Gary. Attack was always the best form of defence. "And you know what I'm talking about."

"Gary, I thought you wanted a baby as much as I do?"

"I do," said Gary. "But it's taking over our lives. I know that it's all that you think about."

"Isn't it the same for you? Don't you want to be a Dad?"

"You know the answer to that, Debs."

"Well, it doesn't seem like it," said Debbie. "I feel like I'm this on my own in this, most of the time."

"I sometimes feel like I'm some kind of stud service," said Gary.

Debbie stepped closer to him. "I'm sorry you feel that way. I didn't know."

"Well, you wouldn't because you've never asked me," said Gary. "But look at what it's doing to us. There's tension in the air all the time."

"I need a baby, Gary. I need a child of our own."

"But what if it doesn't happen, Debbie? Will you be happy with just me?"

"It will happen, Gary!" Debbie insisted.

"But what if it doesn't?"

"But it will! And look, don't drink any beer at the barbecue. I told you it can affect your fertility, just like coffee."

"I'll do whatever I can to get you pregnant, Debbie," said Gary, who'd seen that look on her face many times before. It was the look she gave him whenever she feared she might not get exactly what she wanted and it would all be his fault. It was always his fault when she didn't get what she wanted, whether it was or not. Except this wasn't about a new car or that house she wanted. This was about something much more risky but, even so, he couldn't keep on being subjected to her obsession getting the better of her. "But I don't believe all these old wives tales. I'll have one beer, maybe two. And that won't make any difference at all to when and if you get pregnant."

Debbie slapped his face and then stormed off upstairs.

"It's going to be another nice relaxing Sunday then?" he called after her.

Rebecca came back from the supermarket with four bottles of wine and a couple of large bags of nachos. In her imagination, this was a normal Sunday that she would be spending with Jeff but she knew that the reality was that he'd only agreed to go out on a date with her and see where they go from there. But she'd been waiting so long just to get this far that, for now, it was enough to keep her happy and she was relieved that her journey here to finally confront the issue hadn't resulted in a complete disaster. She put the bottles of white wine in the fridge and then joined Jeff at the barbecue where she placed the bottles of red wine next to the bowls of salad.

"Thanks for all of that," said Jeff. He couldn't help but feel a bit awkward. It was true that he'd been denying his feelings for Rebecca for a long time but it wasn't like flicking a switch. They still had to work together after all and his instincts were still telling him to be cautious.

"Those prawns look lovely," said Rebecca. "And so do the burgers. You're obviously not a bad cook."

"Didn't you already know that, DI Stockton?" he teased.

"Of course," said Rebecca, blushing. "I've always known you're perfect at everything, Detective Superintendent Barton."

"That's what I like to hear."

"I know we shouldn't really talk shop this afternoon but …. Joe Briers?"

"What about him?"

"Well, I'm still getting my head round the fact that he was driven so crazy with resentment over his wife refusing him access to his daughter that he killed, or rather executed, those members of the Gorton Boys and Melanie Patterson."

"Well, I hope his wife is pleased with herself, knowing what her petty little power games led to," said Jeff. "But she's not the first and she won't be the last. You can be sure of that."

"Jeff, I'm really glad that I did the right thing coming over here today."

"Becky, I've been abysmally slow on the uptake," Jeff confessed. "And I'm sorry for that. But yeah, you did the right thing."

"I just want to say though, Jeff…….. well, I just want to ask you really….."

"Ask me what?"

"Well, you won't just play along with me, will you? I mean, you won't mess with my head like that?"

"No, Becky," said Jeff. "I'd never do that to you."

Rebecca smiled. "Thanks. Now, where's that red wine?"

Lucy and Jeff Barton's sister, Annabel, fell into a comfortable friendship almost as soon as they'd been introduced. Jeff thought it was great that his sister would already have a friend on the street when she moved in and he walked over to the corner of the garden where they were sat together, bonding over a bottle of New Zealand Sauvignon Blanc.

"You girls look like you're stirring a witch's cauldron over here," he joked.

"No, we're saving that until Debbie gets here," said Lucy.

Jeff tut-tutted. He knew there was no love lost between those two. "Naughty."

"No, truthful," said Lucy. "But we were actually talking about the only fit-looking single man on the street."

"Oh, and who's that?"

Lucy stuck her tongue out at him. "Not you, so don't flatter yourself."

"Ooh, you're so wounding. I'm off to cook some more sausages."

"And were you interested in my brother?" Annabel asked, after Jeff had gone back to the barbecue.

"I was, yeah," Lucy admitted whilst she checked her phone for text messages. Her son Bradley had sent her one an hour ago saying he was getting the bus home. She sent him one back telling him to come straight to Jeff's barbecue. He should've been here ages ago. She sent him another text asking where he'd got to but she hadn't had a reply to that one. It was unusual for Bradley. He was normally pretty good at returning texts.

"I take it you and this Debbie are not bosom pals?"

"She's the most Stepford of all the Stepford wives round here," said Lucy, helped along in her revelations by another gulp of wine. "She's smug. She definitely looks down on me but then they're all a bit like that round here. I'm definitely the outsider."

"They all sound delightful."

"They piss me off, the lot of them," said Lucy. "They've all been lucky and found someone who wanted to share their life with them. But I've never even come close to that. I don't really know anything about looking after a husband because I've never had one. I've had a few of other people's but I've never had one of my own!"

Annabel laughed. "You terror. That's how I lost my ex-husband."

"Oh, look I'm sorry, I … "

"Don't be, don't be, I'm not going to judge you. Especially as I'm now doing the same with someone else's husband."

"Getting your own back?."

"Not really," said Annabel, who felt a little twitch down below when she thought of her lover Dermot. "I fancy the arse off him and the sex is fantastic."

"Same as me and mine there."

"So I'm just having myself some fun."

"I just wish it could go further, you know?"

"Oh, Lucy, love," said Annabel who sympathised with her new best friend. Such a pretty girl and yet so lonely and in need. "What about Bradley's father? What happened there?"

"He's the same married guy I'm seeing now," Lucy revealed.

"Really?"

"Oh, yes. We had an affair a few years ago. It finished because he was getting guilty about his wife. We lost touch and then, years later, our paths crossed again and we couldn't stop ourselves."

"Does he know that Bradley is his son?"

"No," said Lucy. "That's a little bomb I haven't detonated yet."

When Debbie arrived with Gary, they were holding hands as they walked through to the back garden. Debbie made straight for Lucy after telling Gary not to have a beer.

"Lucy, I noticed that your lounge curtains aren't quite closing at the top in the middle," said Debbie, her face full of fake concern. "And since you're only renting the property and not actually owning it, I sent an email to Brian and Isobel in Dubai to explain that you'd be getting in touch about repairs."

"You did what?"

"Well, I thought I'd save you the job."

"But do you walk down the street looking at everyone else's curtains?"

"Well, no, but then they all own their properties so it's their business."

"You never miss a bloody trick, do you?"

"I beg your pardon?"

"Don't play the innocent. I just feel sorry that you feel you have to pick on me in order to feel better about yourself."

"This conversation is over."

"Are you pregnant yet? That's where I can go one better than you because I've got my Bradley and all you've got are negative test results."

Although Annabel thought that Lucy may be going a bit far she couldn't help but smile. This Debbie woman obviously really got to her.

"Watch your mouth, lady."

Lucy stood and squared up to her adversary. "Why? What are you going to do if I don't?"

"Ladies, please," said Jeff. "Come on now, everyone is here just to enjoy the afternoon."

"I've got more dignity than to get into a fight with you," said Debbie, ignoring Jeff's plea.

"You may have dignity but you still haven't got a baby," Lucy snarled.

"Oh, you really are low," said Debbie who was frustrated that she felt like crying. She didn't want to give this common tart the satisfaction.

"And it's my business to sort any repairs out with my landlord," said Lucy, emphatically. God, she hated this sanctimonious cow. "And you only contacted them to make me feel small and not as good as you and everyone else."

"Well, you're really showing off your common side now aren't you," said Debbie. She glanced round. They were playing to an audience. The garden was full of Jeff's neighbours and they were now being treated to a show. "What do you know about fitting into an area of decent people like this?"

"I know that your husband has got a scar just above his groin. Is that where you cut his balls off years ago?"

Debbie was about to lunge for Lucy with her fists when Rebecca grabbed her from behind and pulled her away.

"I think you'd better go home and calm down, sweetheart," said Rebecca.

"Me? I'm being asked to leave? I'm not the street bike here!"

"Debbie, come on, we're going home where we can talk," said Gary who couldn't believe what had just played out. Lucy had outed their affair and it was going to drive Debbie crazy.

Annabel then pulled Lucy back from going for Debbie and Gary took hold of Debbie's arm. . Debbie screamed for Gary to let go and take his hand off her. She said he disgusted her but it only made him grip her arm tighter. Jeff shook his head in mild amusement at what was happening but was wondering where Toby and the boys had got to. He decided that if they weren't back soon he'd call Lewis on his mobile to see where they'd got to.

"Jeff?" Debbie appealed. "Are you really taking her side over mine?"

"Go home and calm down, Debbie," said Jeff, who knew that Debbie had been in full provocation mode towards Lucy who'd fallen for it good and proper. "I'll see you later."

At that moment the front door burst open and Seamus, the partner of Jeff's brother Lewis, almost fell into the house, out of breath.

"Seamus?" said Jeff. "What's wrong? Where's Toby and the others?"

"They're following. Toby is pretty upset."

"Why? What's happened?"

"We took the long way back from the park," Seamus began to explain as he got his breath back. "Through the woods, by the river, and that's where we found the body. It's of a child, Jeff. Toby found it. That's why he's so upset."

"Oh, my God," said Annabel as everyone else gasped and sighed. "Poor little Toby."

"You'd better come with me, Jeff."

"I'll come too," said Rebecca.

Jeff asked Annabel to look after things at the house and told her he'd call when he knew anything whilst Rebecca called the incident in and asked Control to send a team to the woods. Then the two of them went with Seamus and, once they were a little way down the street, Seamus turned to Jeff and said "I didn't like to say in there with all the folks listening and all, Jeff, especially Lucy....."

"Why? What's Lucy got to with this?"

"The body we found ... well its Bradley, Jeff. It's Lucy's son Bradley."

Meanwhile, David has also begun a series of mystery novels featuring the private investigator Stephanie Marshall and set in Sydney, Australia. The first novel in the series is called *"What Happened to Liam?"* and is available now through all the usual retailers, including Amazon, Kobo, Google etc.

.

Printed in Great Britain
by Amazon